The

BLEEDING

SCARS

John Monyjok Maluth

Copyrighted © 2021 John Monyjok Maluth

All rights reserved.

***

Discipleship Press

Website: www.discipleshippress.wordpress.com
Email: maluthabiel@gmail.com
Phone: +254 797 624 994
+211 927 145 394

~~***~~

P.O. Box 28448-00100, Nairobi Kenya

ISBN: 9798409933838

Library of Congress Control Number: 2022907953

All rights reserved. No part of this book may be reproduced, stored in a retrieval system, or transmitted in any or by any means – electronic, mechanical, photocopying, recording, or otherwise-without prior permission in writing from the publisher.

DISCLAIMER

This is a work of **fiction**. Names, characters, businesses, places, events, locales, and incidents are either the products of the author's imagination or used in a fictitious manner. Any resemblance to actual persons, living or dead, or actual events is purely coincidental. February 13, 2022.

CONTENTS

CHAPTER 1 1
   April 7th 2019, Juba 1

CHAPTER 2 10
   August 18th 1955, Torit 10

CHAPTER 3 18
   April 7th 2019, Nimule 18

CHAPTER 4 26
   May 16th 1983, Malakal 26

CHAPTER 5 34
   August 8th 2019, Adjumani, Uganda 34

CHAPTER 6 42
   April 21st 1997, Khartoum, Sudan 42

CHAPTER 7 50
   August 9th 2019, Maaji 50

CHAPTER 8 58
   January 26th 1989, Nasir 58

CHAPTER 9 67
   August 17th 2019, Maaji II 67

CHAPTER 10 76

February 27th 1972, Addis Ababa 76

CHAPTER 11 84
August 17th 2019, Maaji III 84

CHAPTER 12 92
September 10th 2019, OPM, Adjumani 92

CHAPTER 13 98
March 6th 1993, Wijin, South Sudan 98

CHAPTER 14 106
September 16th 2019, Nimule 106

CHAPTER 15 114
February 12th 1998, Nasir 114

CHAPTER 16 122
September 16th 2019, Nimule 122

CHAPTER 17 130
May 16th 1998, Kiech Kuon 130

CHAPTER 18 138
October 16th 2019, Juba 138

CHAPTER 19 146
November 26th 2006, Malakal 146

CHAPTER 20 154
November 21st 2015, Kampala 154

CHAPTER 21 162
April 4th 2012, Panthou, South Sudan 162

CHAPTER 22 170
July 16th 2011, Kakuma, Kenya 170

CHAPTER 23 178
November 12th 2019, Juba 178

CHAPTER 24 186
June 6th 2011, Bor, South Sudan 186

CHAPTER 25 194
December 15th 2013, Juba 194

CHAPTER 26 202
July 16th 2015, Yambio 202

CHAPTER 27 210
November 28th 2020, Loki, Kenya 210

CHAPTER 28 218
July 16th 2017, Abwong, South Sudan 218

CHAPTER 29 226
March 19th 2020, Juba 226

CHAPTER 30 234
July 16th 2011, Rumbek, South Sudan 234

OTHER BOOKS BY JOHN MONYJOK MALUTH 242

CHAPTER 1

April 7th 2019, Juba

It was on the first Sunday in April, when the thick black clouds formed over Juba, the then capital city. Just a day earlier, I planned and then decided to leave the country, traveling by road to the Ugandan border, hoping to see my wife and children for the first time in six years since the war broke out in the country on the 15th December 2013.

"How far is it to Nimule?" I asked a bus driver who was on his usual military uniforms. Several passengers were looking at me in surprise mode. Some seemed to know the answers to my question. Others wanted to hear from the driver himself. For some, it wasn't their first time to go down that road. But for me and a few others, it was our turn to travel to that part of the country.

"It depends on the road security and the speed we use. Mostly, it takes about 4-5 hours of driving," said the driver. He then left us to call his conductor.

At 7:30a.m, all passengers boarded the bus for Nimule, the bordering town by then between South Sudan and Uganda. As usual, we have already delayed for ten minutes. Most passengers on board were women of different ages from all over the country. They were from all walks of life. However, there were some men like myself, traveling with us for various reasons. Some were soldiers in civilian's clothes. Others were businessmen and businesswomen. Some were on a mission similar to mine: to see their wives and children.

"This is the only tarmac road in the country. How many years now since our independence?" wondered Gatluak, one of the few men on board.

"If you have not started the rebellion the second time, we would have several tarmac roads by now, linking our country to other neighbouring countries. But because you lack vision, we only have this one in the whole of our country," explained Monyluak, another passenger after trying to answer Gatluak's question, which was not even directed to him.

"Both of you love war more than you love peace. If only you have not taken the country backward, we would have many tarmac roads by now. But because we are peaceful, we have at least this one tarmacked road to Uganda," explained Lowila before Gatluak could comment on or answer to Monyluak's points.

"How long will you people stop blaming each other about the past? How long will you men forgive and try to forget those bad historical events? I know we have done all kinds of wrong things to each other in this country. However, if we need peace, we have to find at least one factor for unity," explained Nyamal, one of the women passengers on board, sitting right behind me. I was still listening to them quietly. Her voice was calm, professional, and promising a peaceful heart of a woman, a mother's.

"You people are the main cause of the problem. You keep going back to the 1991 events, but you started the war within the movement in 1983. You hijacked the leadership, and then killed the movement's true leader. You have committed many atrocities. We all know our history. You are the problem, not us," Gatluak answered at last. He was responding to Monyluak's comments, adding some historical facts that his meagre memory could recall.

"You rebelled three times. Instead, we only did it once. You did it first in 1991, and again in 2013. You have been on the enemy's side ever since 1956. And then again in 2016, you planned to kill the country's president, just to take over the national power by force so that you have your big share in the national cake. But it didn't work, because as we say in our language, the government has a long hand," Monyluak went on.

"Someone said, 'there's no smoke without fire,' and that's very true to me. We didn't rebel for nothing, ya Monyluak. You either don't want to admit the truth, since you people don't possess the truth, or you just don't know anything about our national history. We knew from the very beginning that you won't be able to lead this country responsibly and peacefully," Gatluak went on.

"May you people change the topic now?" Lowila asked, looking at Monyluak on his left, and then Gatluak on his right.

"You people must join at least one side. You better join us so that we fight against this regime," lamented Gatluak.

"We can't and we won't join any madness! We have already fought for this country. If you don't stop this senseless war sooner, we will join hands to fight against both of you. If we succeed, we will then break off and join the Ugandan people. We will then be Ugandans!" roared the angered Lowila.

"Yes, you are welcome to Uganda!" shouted Julia, a Ugandan female passenger on board.

"We're not, and we'll never become Ugandans, or even East Africans, just because we aren't, naturally. We better be Sudanese instead," Obaj, one of the few South Sudanese men on board objected.

"Lowila, can you see how you and your people always want to sell our country cheaply to both Uganda and Sudan? We're not Ugandans or Kenyans.

We're not even Sudanese, or Ethiopians. We are but South Sudanese," Gatluak spoke up again.

"Yes, Gatluak. Now you're talking. I agree with you on that one thing. These guys don't know the differences between us and other nationalities. That's why they nicknamed us MTN. They ambushed and killed innocent women and children on our national roads, just because they can't fight either the government or the rebels," Monyluak went on.

"You always agree and then disagree on almost anything. You people are sick. What you have in your heads is a cow's brain. If you have human brains, at least you would have known the fact that hatred and killings are not the way to build a nation," Lowila spoke up his heart.

"Who ambushes cars and kills innocent women and children on our roads? Is it not you, the Equatorial citizens? Is it Nuer or Dinka who kill people on the roads in cool blood? You people are not men," Monyluak jumped right in.

I could see that I and the women were now silenced by these men in rage. They were about to box themselves on the bus if they could only get closer enough to each other.

"It's better for Sudan to reunite once and forever. We can't govern ourselves if we think and speak like this. It's much better for the Arabs to govern us, or if not, the UN Trusteeship is the next option," Obaj said. He spoke under his voice as if he was speaking to himself, not wanting anyone to hear what he was saying. I could resonate. His points were hurting, but at least he spoke out loud enough for all of us to hear.

"You too are like these idiots. You want us to be under someone else's power. This is why you rebelled against the movement in 1991, forming your own movement in Nasir. But the strong and mighty SPLA defeated you all the so called SPLA-Nasir faction," Monyluak responded.

"The division came about as a result of your failure in leadership. No one wanted to rebel against you if at all you were leaders and not rulers. History tells it all. You people have a different mentality when it comes to leadership. Do you listen to your very own artist who says that leadership is not like going into a dancing party hall? Do you all believe that you were born to rule?" Obaj questioned.

"Tell him, Obaj. At least you seem to know our history. Nothing is hidden in this world. For sure, some of those people you mistreated are still alive to tell the story. Who doesn't know your mistreatment, Monyluak? Do you think the world doesn't know you yet? You're always the cause of all the chaos in this country from the very beginning. We all know this. Today, your leaders keep reminding us that they fought for this country, therefore, they have all the rights to grab lands and commit all kinds of atrocities. But this is a white lie. All of us participated in the liberation struggle. Do you understand?" Gatluak questioned, looking at Monyluak in the eyes.

"Yes, all of us participated in the liberation struggle. In fact, we started the liberation struggle. Do you people even know what Anya-nya means? This is an equatorial name. Do you understand? It's a Madi word, which means 'snake poison,'" Lowila explained.

"Oh, okay. You mean you know the real history of this country? Why are you then hiding in the bushes to shoot and kill only civilians if you are real men? Even in those days, you only poisoned the Arabs with that snake venom and you think you fought them? This is called *Luch* in my language. It means to kill someone without his knowledge. Real men fight head-on, but can you?" Gatluak questioned.

"You mean your language resembles mine? We call it the same when you kill someone in cold blood and you make sure no one else knows about the killing. This is sinful. Real men fight face-to-face. This is how we fight," Monyluak agreed.

"What did Moses do in the Bible? Maybe you don't even have bibles in your languages. Do you know that sometimes you have to fight by all means in order for you to win the war? Moses killed an

Egyptian to save his countryman. But when this was known, Moses fled the land for forty years. It's better to be wise," Lowila went on to explain his points. Each of them wanted to speak for his tribe instead of speaking for his country.

"Lowila, this is how coward people behave. We understand. Keep doing that even today. But that won't help you or the country, will it?" Gatluak asked, turning his attention to Lowila, who was sitting in the middle.

And then suddenly, silence fell on us as if someone commanded it. We were in the most dangerous spot where unknown gunmen may attack any moving vehicle at any time, at will.

The driver and most of the passengers knew it well because some of them survived the attacks sometimes back. But as quietness returned, I meditated on the words I have just heard on the same public bus.

All I could see was a nation divided along tribal lines. It was very clear to me that the wounds of the first two Sudanese wars were not yet scars, or worse still, those scars may bleed at any time, should anyone dare to scratch on them.

But this was only the beginning. The worst was yet to come as I went places to listened to our people. It doesn't matter where you go, you will always see the bleeding scars.

Is there a way to heal our country?

CHAPTER 2

August 18th 1955, Torit

Growing up under the guardianship of my fraternal grandfather, Nhial, I always wanted to know something about our country's history, first hand. Nhial was one of the first liberation struggle soldiers, a well-known veteran from 1955-1972, which ended with the Addis Ababa Agreement, in Ethiopia, signed between GOS and the SSLM on 27th March 1972. He always told us stories about how the Anya-Nya I's (a Madi word for a 'snake venom') movement failed. Joseph Lagu was the leader of that first liberation movement. According to oral stories, he was then bribed with a beautiful Arab girl, so that he could accept to sign the deceitful peace agreement between Juba and Khartoum.

Before the Anya-Nya I's reintegration into the Sudanese government, Samuel Gach Tut and his comrades of the then Anya-Nya II refused to sign the fragile peace deal in 1972. They remained in the bush until the time came when the young educated man, Dr. John Garang de Mabior, joined them in the Thiajak Village to the Ethiopian border in the east. Akuot Atem was one of the prominent leaders of this movement. But because of his educational level, Garang took over the leadership after killing Samuel

Gach Tut, making his way to the then leadership of the Ethiopian government. That was how he became a prominent leader of the new movement, the Sudan People's Liberation Movement/Army, (SPLM/A).

He told me about all the events, especially how Samuel was killed, and how Dr. Garang became the only suitable leader of the SPLM/A, communicating with the outside world. He told me how the SPLM/A was made up of mostly communism ideologies, resulting in the godlessness and lawlessness in the SPLM/A in those early years of the movement's life.

He told me how the Nuer people became very bitter about the events, and how they rebelled against the new movement's leadership ever since, forming the Anya-Nya II of which he became a member. He told me about many other atrocities committed by the new regime against the Nuer along the way. The Nuer youth then armed themselves and attacked the SPLM/A, which was then mainly made up of the Dinka tribe where the new leader came from.

Nhial said their main agenda was to liberate the south from the north, so that we can then achieve our independence. He said their aim was to set their country men and women free from the Arab bondage. Their agenda was not the New Sudan, but the new country called South Sudan, Azania, or Cush. He said if they succeeded to create a new nation, whatever name that comes from the citizens could be considered by the leadership of the new country. He told me about many internal senseless wars that were between the main peoples of the country, the major tribes. He always spoke, blaming the other party, the other side of the war. He thought all the faults were not theirs but Dinka's.

However, my maternal uncle was always very different. He had his own side of the story. He always tells me about all the atrocities the Nuer people have ever since committed against the Dinka people in particular, and the movement at large. However, he never denied the fact that the Dinkas also have treated the Nuers with contempt and even with persecution. He told me how William Nyuon's bodyguards were literally killed in his absence because of the direct orders by his colleagues in the army such as comrade Kuol Manyang Juuk.

He always admits that Nyuon was forced into rebellion because of the atrocities committed against his Nuer bodyguards, and nothing was done about it by the top leadership of the then SPLM/A. But, he never denied the fact that he will never forget what the Nuers did in a form of the revenge attacks and the killings of the innocent Dinka people in the villages in the Upper Nile region. These two men were from the Nuer people with different ideas and thoughts. They had different points of view about the same issues relating to the history of the new country. Each had a point to make, so I had to listen to them as much as I could. Each had a view. They may look at the same coin and see it differently based on their worldviews.

On the other side of the civil war, I also had an uncle and a cousin brother. They also had their views about both the Nuer and the Dinka people. Deng, my maternal uncle believes that Nuers are to be blamed for every bad thing that hurts South Sudan as a nation. This to him was because as Dr. Garang said in one of his present speeches, the Nuer has stabbed us from the back. On the other hand, my elder cousin brother thinks each of the two people groups, the main tribes in the country according to the population numbers, are to be blamed at some degree. He mostly pointed fingers at the other section of the Dinka people, the Bahr el Ghazal. But to my amazement, Bahr el Ghazal is only a region, not a tribe.

Garang, my elder cousin brother accuses the Dinka of Bahr el Ghazal of looting the national resources ever since we were still in the bush. He thinks and voices his concerns that these people are even worse than the Nuer who killed his relatives. He told me one day that the other section of the Dinka people can do anything for a personal gain. He had his own words that my mouth can't be able to speak out. My hands can't even write them down. The words were too heavy for my fingers to type. They are hard to the point that my keyboard can't type them.

But memory is funny. I can remember most of the words he used when blaming the other side. This tells me that people have their own opinions about anything. It reminds me that we can't generalize people by a tribe or people group. We may be wrong to say all Dinka people agree to do this or that. We may be wrong to think that all Nuer or Nyam-nyam (Equatorians) people are the same. Why is it so? It is so because people are always different, not only from their appearances, but from their inner most beings, their minds.

I, Mut Peter, have come up with my own ways of analysing issues that are facing our nation, South Sudan. I better do whatever I can instead of pointing a finger at an individual or to a group of people.

One day, we were seated under the tree, my grandpa's tamarind tree, chatting.

"Garang, why do you always feel bad about the Dinka people?" I asked.

"I like the Dinka Padang and the other groups such as the Dinka Bor, but those guys on the west are but thieves. To hell they must go. They will loot this country to the last droplet. They are everywhere. They love using national resources for their own gain," he explained his points, looking at me in the eyes.

"But, are you saying all of them are bad?"

"Yes, most of them are evil, if not all."

"But how do you come to that conclusion?"

"Mut. Let me tell you something. You don't have to do research about everything, and then write reports about it. This doesn't work in the real world. Academic research, which I think you allude to, is only good for academic purposes. I know that these people are very wicked!" he shouted.

"Yeah, I understand your points. But is what you are saying based on facts or is it based on mere beliefs about these people? I know many of our people believe that the Dinka are all carnivores, but this is far from the truth. None of the Dinka tribes have carnivores people in them."

"Well, then you are not normal. What is the reason for you to go to school if you can still be as ignorant as you are? Don't you know that Gatluak Manguel was a Dinka from Lakes State?" he asked.

The conversation heated up in minutes. I had to end it right there because it was going to be endless like an abyss. One is much better to be doing something productive instead of arguing with such people. This is how the scars can still bleed. People truly have beliefs about each other, and these beliefs are always based on bad historical records against each other. I can remember how a small boy asked his father why Mony-nuer was coming to their home. He wanted to know if this was the same Nuer who killed his great grandparents.

Garang was not alone. There are many others like him. They are the way they are because of a reason. You can't manage to talk them out of their beliefs and their real-life experiences.

How long are we going to be and live like this after gaining our independence? Will we ever learn to forgive and then forget the past? It's not possible to forget those terrible events, but we can stop them from happening again in the future, can't we?

But we can only do this if we are ready for it. Being ready means being a coward. It means being a woman. It means being heartless and fearful. It means a lot of negative things we can't even imagine to think about. For people like Nhial, my grandfather, peace is much more important than conflicts.

I have inherited this mindset from him. He is a different man, different from others in his generation. I am different, too. I love peace and harmony. I know that life is not in our hands. This means revenge is not the way out. We must learn from our past, if we want to prevent history from repeating itself. But the fact is that history indeed repeats itself. If our white brothers and sisters couldn't believe we the black have spirits and souls to go heaven, how can we humans accept each other as if we belong to one origin? But we are not the same.

There are peace lovers everywhere. There are trouble makers everywhere as well. They love to fight and kill other people. They are also killed at war in most cases. But the peaceful also die in the process.

I wonder if humans can live in true peace with each other. If human leaders always fake their ways into leadership only to do that which they never said they will, how on earth will people live in true peace with each other? It is always a wonder.

Do you love peace or violence? You have your own reasons for loving either of these. I am not a judge to judge you. We can't be the same. We had to be different. It's the nature's way of doing things. This is because anything that lives also has conflicts either with itself or with others. Even dogs commit suicide. They hate it when they are in trouble.

Animals do fight. Birds and insects fight. Even worms know how to defend themselves from other worms or other creatures. Life is full of conflict. This may be the way of life. But is this normal?

CHAPTER 3

April 7th 2019, Nimule

"Look, even your names are identical, so how do you claim to be different? You love fighting against each other over simple things such as cattle, girls, women, and now you are fighting over the presidential seat! Do you think you are always right?" Lowila goes on, asking his toughest questions that I think deserve an answer.

Before either Gatluak or Monyluak could respond to Lowila's questions, gunshots are starting just ahead of us. It's on the very road we're travelling on. Our driver stops the bus, wanting to know what's going on. The gunshots increase. They seem to be coming closer and closer.

We must wait.

After about half an hour of silence, the driver makes up his mind.

"Get on board!" he shouts.

We all have to hop onto the long bus. Ten minutes later, we reach to the ambush scene. Their blood, faeces, and mucus mingled on the ground and on the attacked bus. The bus driver is shot dead on spot. The wounded are rescued and are being taken ahead of us by an army vehicle, the same that came to their rescue. The ambush was carried out by the usual known yet unknown gunmen and gunwomen, living somewhere unknown to the national military servants. Among the deceased were men, women, and children from different tribes. Some men have marks resembling mine, reminding me of that same fate, would I have been on the same bus. The bus was just ahead of us. I then think of what caused us to delay for ten minutes before we got started from Juba this morning. Was that a plan of God to spare our lives?

The SPLA soldiers were still standing along the road. They motion to our driver, telling him the road ahead is safe. We had to leave the ambush scene, going on with our long unexpected journey. We're all quiet, no words, but we're speaking from within. Humans never keep quiet even when they're sleeping.

"Look, how can real men enjoy killing their own harmless men, women, and children? Didn't I tell you, Lowila that you guys are women in men's clothes?" Gatluak questions. Lowila now seems to be thinking about the most important things. He ignores him. He might have been focusing on the things that are from above instead of the things from below.

"But, Gatluak, are these not your very own terrorists called rebels? Even if they are not from your tribe, are they not fighting for your own course? They do it in the name of the opposition, of which you are the leaders. One day, it will be a family business.

Idiots!" Monyluak questions and then ended his questions with insults. They seemed to have regained courage after a few hours away from the ambush scene. I, Mut Peter, listen on as if absent. I have no interest in such arguments. I have no side to take. I know I was, I am, and I will always be a South Sudanese by birth. I don't deny being a Nuer, biologically, but I seem to have developed a different mentality. I live a higher life, not the normal lower life which most people seem to live.

"None of you have a clue about who these attackers were. They can either be rebels, or just robbers, taking advantage of this time of national crisis. Do you guys see how small you think?" Lowila speaks up at last. He then stares at the green grass by the roadside. He seems to be reflecting on the past events. Maybe he's imagining how safe the road is.

"I told you long ago that blaming each other will not resolve our national issues at all. You men need to sit down and discuss to find out a solution. Do you guys think hatred, either tribal or religious, will save the world?" Nyamal questions Gatluak, Monyluak and Lowila, the three talkative young men on board. They went silent for a while, no answers to her heartily and motherly questions. She speaks like a mother-to-be, a mother of a nation, not of a tribe. She goes on with words and actions that my small mind can't recall as I am reflecting on this many moon months later on after the events. But she was unique and special.

"Listen, Nyamal, what makes you interfere with men's affairs? You're supposed to be quiet as other women are when men speak. I wonder how living in big cities will make women think beyond themselves. Just don't say anything again after this!" Gatluak warns, pointing at Nyamal with his thumb and the middle finger, forgetting that the other three remaining fingers are pointing back at himself.

"Brother, don't you know I am a man with a womb? I also have 25% representation in the government, according to the laws of this land. Also, have I said anything foolish or womanish for that matter?" Nyamal makes her points and then starts questioning Gatluak. Whenever I look at her in the eyes, she smiles back regardless of how furious she was with a young man who seems to be blinded to her wise words.

"She was 100% right. If women should lead this country, we will have no ambushes on our roads. If all your women think like this before they act foolishly, then they are the men. You are the women instead of us being women. We think before we act. We count the cost before we take any actions," Lowila speaks. "I told you earlier that you guys better get to Uganda in order to stop all these issues. Let them remain with their Sudan, and come to the pearl of Africa. You are already Ugandans, but you don't want to fully join us legally. This is the only way to live in peace," Julia suggests.

"Julia, to hell you go with your ideas! Who told you we are Ugandans, Kenyans, Ethiopians, Congolese, or even Sudanese? Look, you still call us Sudanese, are you behind the news that South Sudan became a sovereign state of its own on the 9th of July, 2011?" Monyluak speaks up after a while.

I could see how furious he is against a young beautiful woman who suggests that one main region of his beloved country should be annexed to the southern neighbour.

"Indeed, we are all Sudanese," Obaj objects.

I then take a turn to look at Nyamal. Our eyes meet and then she smiles a second time.

"Why are you not saying a word?" she asked.

"I'm just thinking about my wife and little children. I don't know if I will find them alive and well. I don't know which refugee camp in northern Uganda they are in right now," I explain.

"Oh, are you also a refugee?"

"I am not a refugee, but my wife and children are refugees." "I see. I hope she was from our people. Most tribes in South Sudan have ladies that are not faithful to wait for too long. They want a man besides them each and every night, but we are different. My husband is a soldier. But I make sure I come to Juba to see him after every three years. I am a refugee, too," she goes on.

"Did you say you can wait for a man for two years? Did you mean the whole year of 12 months?" asks Julia.

"Why not? He's mine, and I am his!"

"But does he think like you do?"

"I don't have to think like him. I had to think like me, a woman. I am a daughter of a man and a woman. I had to be faithful to my husband."

"But is he always faithful to you?"

"I know that men don't have to be faithful to their wives, this is something natural. Give him the freedom. By the way, women are not sexy, and that's their nature. He can have as many wives as he wants, but I still love him for the eternity future."

"Then you are not fine. You might be sick. In this world, you have the freedom of choice. For me, I can't wait for a man that long, simply because I know he's not waiting for me. I can't spend a night without a man besides me unless if it is for a good reason," Julia goes on.

Silence again crept into the bus. Everyone seems to be thinking about any possible danger ahead. Life is so uncertain especially in a country that is used to wars and violence. This conflict has been there for years. It can happen between to people, or between two groups of people, or tribes. Peace is only a dream in the minds of many people like myself.

"Why are you silent, Lowila? Can you talk now? You've seen what your idiots have done, didn't you? How can real men kill innocent civilians in such a cowardice manner?" wonders Gatluak.

"You're much better than them, man. At least you can fight with your lives. But these guys can't manage to attack their real enemy. Instead, they attack their very own civilians. Did you not hear that some of the dead in that bus are actually their people? A bus is a house that all kinds of people enter. It's not made of one or two tribes," Monyluak joins the talk.

"Who told you the killers are from my tribe? Don't you know that Equatoria is simply a region with many other tribes in it? It's not like your Upper Nile, or Bahr el Ghazal, where only one tribe lives in a region. For us, we welcome every human into our homeland and this includes foreigners," Lowila speaks up again after those painful words directed at him.

"I think you're right. But each region is made up of more than one tribe. This means both the Upper Nile and Bahr el Ghazal are also made up of more than Nuer and the Dinka," I join the conversation between the three young men for the first time.

They're both looking at me now with some kind of surprise on their faces. Do they also judge me by how I look? Are they seeing my facial scarification markings?

"Are you from the Upper Nile?" asks Lowila.

"Can't you tell by just looking at his face?" Gatluak jumps in.

"He's my cousin. I can tell by looking at the marks on his forehead. Good enough, we the younger generations don't have such marks anymore. I can tell, he's older than all of us here. Maybe he's your age mate, Lowilia. It's hard to tell how old you people may be. You all look too short but huge. You seem to be expanding every year. But for us, we stretch upward. Maybe that's why you can't fight real men because you resemble women," Gatluak resumes.

At this point, I don't want to comment. It's getting to my nerves. Commenting on his judgments isn't a solution. Rather, it's another problem to deal with. I can see how we're still scratching on these old wounds. I can see how we think. At the moment, I am remembering how a tribe could fight against itself. The Mundari people are killing themselves for no good reason. But could there be any reason for anything in this life? Is life not just what it is?

CHAPTER 4

May 16th 1983, Malakal

"Look, you must learn more about your young nation's history. I know a lot of it, my grandson," Nhial told me. He's still very strong and lively. He's saying this while spreading his cow dung for the sun to dry it up. Cow dung was used as fuel to make an undesirable smoke, not only bad for humans, but for causing the flies to fly away. The smoke from the dung scared away other insects that are to feed on the cattle, including ticks and houseflies.

"Who started the liberation struggle, the Nuer or the Dinka?" I asked. "We, the mighty Nuer started it. Before Jaden, Mourtat, and Lagu, we had the idea of the independence or to a federal state of South Sudan, or Cush Republic. But they hijacked it from us in 1983. They killed our leader and then installed theirs. This is why we fight them to this day. But as the Prophet Ngundeng Bong used to say that "the goodness and the badness of the world starts from the Nuer," we will still rule this country, one day," he went on. I had no idea if he was referring to the Anya-Nya II movement, or the Anya-Nya I. If he meant the latter, then I would surely disagree with him almost on the spot. If he meant the former, then he was right because this second movement was mainly made up of the Nuer fighters who were then disappointed by the Addis Ababa Agreement's outcomes. I had no interest in his Ngundeng tales. I had no idea about who that old prophet was and his messages. I wondered if he was from God, or from Satan. But I swallowed my pride and thoughts. I didn't believe in either God or Satan.

"Who was then the first leader of the struggle before the Dinka took away the leadership from you?" I asked. "There were many of them, but Samuel Gach Tut was one of them. He was one of the prominent leaders that they later on murdered in cool blood. Do you think we are angered against the Dinka for nothing?" he answered with a question, looking at me in the eyes before he walked away. After he returned, I had to resume the talk.

"Tell me, how did Garang take over the leadership? What was the name of the second movement after the Anya-Nya?" I asked while walking behind him before we both reached to the shade under his personal tamarind tree, the one he planted in the then Rupkoni Village long before my father was born.

"The young man did it after Joseph Lagu instructed him to go to a military school in the USA, and then he came back to Sudan. He then asked for an official visit to South Sudan and then he rebelled against the government on the way. He passed through Dinka Ngok land until he reached to where we were by then to the border of Ethiopia. I was there when he arrived. I was with the late Gach Tut and the rest of our leaders," he went on with the story. "His car's wreckages can still be found in the Kany-beek Village, which is one of the villages between Lou Nuer and the Dinka Ngok areas," he went on.

Grandpa told me how Garang had an agreement with those of General William Nyuon Bany. Nyuon then rebelled in Ayod, managing to take away his 104 battalion. He killed several enemy **soldiers and a few** officers. Little did he know that a few years later, he and his own bodyguards, will be the first victims of the very liberation movement, the very one he was fighting for like a lioness. I was told he was then mistreated before he boldly started to walk away from the main movement during a broad daylight.

"Where did Dr. John Garang get his support from, militarily?" I asked. "Well, he became a communist in order to get support from the Ethiopian government, which was then a communist government. That was the reason why Garang preached that he never seen a nation going to either a church or a mosque. He wanted to separate religion from the state," he went on. I could easily locate some of those speeches of the late Dr. John Garang on the YouTube website today to confirm my grandpa's words. This is the power of technology, isn't it? It is. We can check historical facts online these days.

"What happened next after this?" I asked. "Well, Garang changed his mind when the Soviet Union was on the brink of collapsing, and that was in 1989, so he became a Christian instead, winning the American trust. He then told the world that he was fighting a religious war to liberate the Christian-African south from the Arab-Muslim north. This cunning and then wise tactic brought about all the Western support to the SPLA/M until the signing of the Comprehensive Peace Agreement (CPA) in the Nyayo Stadium in Nairobi, Kenya in 2005," he went on. I can't catch it. It's like a dream during the day.

"You mean he (Garang) was not a Christian in the first place?" I asked, looking at him in the eyes to show how desperate I was to know his answer. The old man looked away before answering.

"No, he was a Christian before that. But his main goal to switch from the SU to the US was to win the Western trust. He needed support, nothing more, nothing less. And, I think he was right, wasn't he?" he questioned after explaining his heartfelt points to answer my deepest questions. He then looked at my face and smiled. But his answer relieved my doubts and my head stopped rolling from the inside, and I think he knew what the hell was going on within my mind. As we talk, my mind wanders to other parts of the story, going back and forth in it. I had to remember almost everything the old man is saying besides note-taking, which is but another lesson to learn as well. Note-taking is never my best career, but things like these are worth-learning, aren't they?

"If Dr. Garang de Mabior was such a wise man, who only used the world's superpowers of the day for his own good or gain, is that the reason we are still keeping both China and the United States of America as our allies or as friends at the same time? Why are we not telling the truth as a country? Why are we not taking one and let the other go?" I thought to myself for a while.

"What do you think about Christianity?"

"I think it is a foreign idea. It's a foreign religion, which has contributed a lot in spoiling our culture and lifestyle. It came with the so called capitalism mind-set where an individual doesn't mind about others that much. This is not human but animal life," he answered.

"How does Christianity contribute in spoiling our African, South Sudanese, or even Nuer cultures?" "Christianity in itself is just a philosophy. But that was either misrepresented by the Western missionaries, who by themselves had their own cultures and traditions besides Christianity, or by our very own people misunderstood it altogether. We were told that everything spiritual in Africa is evil or satanic. This led to the young people not to be listening to their parents because they think their parents are primitive and evil. The children were confused between these two different worlds," he went on to explain his points.

"Well, I think you are right, if I understood the points you made. Does this mean that Christianity in itself is not the problem but the people who brought it, or those who then received it?"

"Exactly. But the concept itself is not natural to us here in Africa. For example, the Westerners don't marry more than one wife for their own reasons. One reason is economic challenges, and the other is human jealousy. Their wives are so selfish that they can't accept each other to be married to one man, even if he is able to feed them. They better stay single forever than to get married to a man with other wives," he explained.

"Is that not an insult to the Americans who helped us because we lied to them that we are Christians?" "No, it's not an insult. Some of us are Christians, but not me. I can't be a Christian. I believe in God in my African way," he said. "What's that African way?"

"It's how I see God. He's the cause of both good and evil in the world, just because He alone can do this. There's nothing like Satan or the Devil. These are realities, but they're not personalities. There're no good or evil angels. There're no fallen angels. There's no heaven or hell. These are human concepts. We do have the same concepts even here in Africa. But we don't personalise evil or good. They're all works of God."

"Why do you love pointing fingers at others?"

"I do this because it's part of the evolutionary memory in me. I don't even know I am doing just that in most cases. I feel like I am expressing myself, trying to make a valuable point. You are the same, my son. Don't tell me you don't blame yourself, church, friends, colleagues, co-works, parents, siblings, nature, and even God. We all have those habits."

"The Bible says there're both hell and heaven!"

"I don't care what it says. Do you believe the book fell from heaven? Even the Quran itself was edited and corrected over the years. None of these great human books are directly from the skies above. Again, everything it says is exactly what it teaches. Do you agree that polygamy is biblical?"

"Yes, the Bible mentions people who got married to more than one wife at the same time. But their lives were always terrible. This means it's not a good practice. Do you agree that the Bible mentions it but it's not teaching us to do this?" I am looking at the old man now in the eyes, but he seems not to be interested in my gestures. He doesn't want to get the same reactions I am going through right now. "You're right. It doesn't teach us to get married to more than one wife today. But also it doesn't say that it's evil."

"But Paul said it's good to get married to only one wife in 1st Corinthians 7!"

"Read that chapter again and try to understand it from its context. This is not a new mistake. Many people are making these mistakes every day. It's just an error. He never said one wife or one husband for that matter, but you assumed he did. Listen, Paul said a lot of things that are purely his thoughts. Thus, they're not the Word of God. They're his human thoughts. Sometimes, he admits this very clearly."

"When God created Adam, he created one Eve for him. Is this not a sign that He wants us to get married to only one wife in our lifetime?"

"If you can do that, then it's fine. But don't impose this idea into other people because God made them different from you. God never condemned polygamy in any way in the Bible. It's up to you and me to decide whether it's good or evil. Period."

CHAPTER 5

August 8th 2019, Adjumani, Uganda

In the following morning after I spent the night in Nimule at a friend's home, I had to restart the journey to Adjumani District in the northern part of Uganda, the neighbouring country to South Sudan. Again, on that minibus were South Sudanese from all directions, ages, genders, and walks of life.

"How far is it from here to Adjumani?" I asked a passenger, whose name I didn't know yet at that stage. "I am not sure how far it is, it's my first time to go there from here. But my elder sister may tell us how far it is from here," she explained.

"Just the same distance like that from here to Juba," answered one of the stand-by passengers, waiting for the minibus to get full. This was long before the deadliest COVID-19 pandemic infected the world, so the bus must be full to its capacity. When the bus was full, we had to jump in, and the driver took his seat, and the journey kicked off. A few minutes later after the journey started, the same conversation as that of the day before started. Most of the passengers on board were women and girls. I missed my first co-passengers. They might have been taking different vehicles altogether.

"Where are you going?" Abuk, one of the women passengers seated on my left, just next to me asked, looking at me in the eyes.

"I am going where you are going," I responded. "But do you know where I am going?" she asked before faking a smile. Grownups know exactly the difference between a fake smile and the real one. They know it from many different gestures and clues, such as the tone of voice, and the body language.

"I guess you are going to one of the refugee camps around the Adjumani District in northern Uganda," I answered. "Sure, but there are many of these camps nowadays, so which one are you going?" she asked again, looking at me right in the eyes. I began to feel uncomfortable at her, but I also have to fake it.

"I am going to the Maaji Refugee Camp," I gave her the shortest answer possible. "Oh, me too, I'm going there. We may just be neighbours, I hope so," she said, now looking away from me at last as if she was done.

"Oh, that's okay if we are neighbours. I don't know where my home is because it's my very first time to take a visit since the war broke out in Juba in 2013," I explained myself.

"Oh, really?" the bus echoed the surprising sounds of almost all the women, the South Sudanese women on board. It seems as if they agreed to say the same thing. I had to remind myself that women have a few amazing characteristics men don't have. For example, they can multitask. They can all speak to each other at the same time, and it always seems that they are able to understand everything. Men can't just do this. They also can laugh at the same time as if they signalled to each other about it.

"You men are not funny at all! See, you are going for a visit after how many years? Six years? If I am your wife, you'll find me with two children from any other man I could find," she went on. I guess she meant it. Her personality tells she can't wait that long, but this wasn't a South Sudanese culture, I thought.

"Are you not saying anything to defend yourself?" Buk asked. I then turned my head backward to have a look at her face, but she then looked away through the car window.

"No, he has nothing to say. What can he say in self-defence when he knows I am right?" Abuk asked. I still went silent. She was too fast that it was hard for me to say a word before she jumps in.

"Well, I think you are all right in your unique ways. We all see the world from our different perspectives, don't we?" I finally broke the silence. The women looked at me from different angles, depending on where each was seated on the minibus. "Men don't care about their wives and children because they are free to marry at any time at will. When a man is in Juba, and his wife is in the refugee camp, he is free to have another wife wherever he is. If this is true, how can men think of their wives when they can find new ones anywhere?" asked Nyapach, one the women on board. Then there was a sense of silence for a few minutes. I didn't know if the question was meant for me, other women, or for her.

"I don't think all men are the same, and all women are not the same, too!" I exclaimed.

"Well, you may be right in your own eyes, but men share some things in common," Abuk answered. I wonder if these women read my thoughts. I remember reading Hill's book, Think and Grow Rich, which said something about thought. The book said thoughts travel from one person to the other. I was thinking that women share some things in common, and here is a woman telling me that men also share some things in common.

"Look," Abuk resumed.

"All men in our country want to fight. They want to kill each other for no apparent reason," she went on. Indeed, I could relate with her on this. It was men who were talking about war just the other day. It was men who attacked the vehicle ahead of us, killing innocent men, women, and children. These were not women. And one of the women on board, Nyamal, was advocating for peace and true reconciliation among men.

"No, it's the Dinka men who love the fighting and the looting of our national resources! We the Nuer are not like this, both our men and our women. We are but peaceful people," Buk, a woman seated at the back seat, objected sharply. She almost jumped out of the window as she tries to make her points heard. But we were not that far away from her. Unless we have hearing issues, we still can hear her loud and clear.

"No, both of you people are but violent. You can even tell by the way you are speaking. Can't you have respect for this man who you don't even know?" asked Kiden, a woman seated right behind my seat.

"What do you mean we are violent? Did you not see those dead innocent civilians on the road yesterday? I saw them and I knew a Nuer man can't kill such angels. I knew the man must be a woman in men's suites!" Buk went on.

"Hey, can you just stop shouting? This is not South Sudan! This is Uganda, okay? If you continue to talk your nonsense, I will stop the car and call the police to take care of you!" shouted the driver, almost losing control of the steering wheel. All the women on board started to scream loud enough, forgetting what the topic of discussion was. Again, I went into my own world of silence, my inner peace. I have seen once again one thing that unites all females, both human and animal: fear.

"How many wives do you have? By the way, you look like a Nuer, aren't you?" Abuk asked two different questions before I could answer the first one. I wondered about what might be going on in her mind at this moment in time.

"I have several wives, woman, but why do you want to know?" I asked. "You see? He said he has several wives. Do you mean all are in the refugee camps? The UN is indeed the father of your children. But are you Nuer or Dinka?" she went on, asking and even answering some of her questions.

"Well, I am kind of a mixture of the two. About my wives, I have one wife in Kakuma, and another in Maaji. The first wife is in Maaji, and the second wife is in Kakuma," I explained.

"But two wives are not several wives, are they?" Buk asked, and the women laughed once again in a unison. I don't know or understand how they do it. A few minutes ago they almost started a fight against each other, and now they are again laughing heartily as if nothing happened at all. This was one of the amazing things I was learning about women.

"I can't be a second wife, never!" Kiden spoke up again before looking through the car window. It's already over two hours since we left Nimule for Adjumani, and we were about to arrive.

"Was that your culture?" Nyapach asked.

Before Kiden could answer, I am already thinking about this world. This world is what it is. It's not that different from the old one. Humans and other things around them are literally the same. I could recall how the same human jealousy kept men and women to fight over each other's bodies.

"No. It's my personality. I didn't say it's our culture not to share a man with another woman. But I think most women don't want to do so even though some bad cultures force them into it. We're now in a free world. We're not supposed to live by our cultures. Do you not understand?" she asked, looking at Abuk in the eyes as if to dictate her thoughts.

"For us, no one forces it on you. It's just natural for a man to have more than one wife. In fact, it's a good thing for a woman to have co-wives in a society. It means we can work together as a team. Our children are one man's children," Abuk goes on.

"When we die, our children remain after us. One woman can't produce enough children compared to two women. This is our culture, and this is natural. This is how the world is. Look, some bird species could have as many wives as they want in their lifetime, and this is okay," Abuk resumes. She was so confident in what she was saying and her tone of voice could tell. Despite the driver's warnings, she keeps going on. She speaks as loud as she could.

Abuk is speaking up her heart. She seemed to have a proper understanding of what she was saying. But was her friend on the same side? I wonder if what she calls natural is truly natural to every other human.

"At least this is not natural to me. I can't be a wife to a man with more than me as a wife. This is not natural. It's a man-made culture, and it's destructive whether you agree with me or not. For our people, it used to be the same many years ago. Some men still cheat when they're hiding other wives somewhere until a time comes for the men to die. This is when other women and children begin to show up," Kiden confesses the wickedness of men on the face of the earth. This is terrible, isn't it?

"If you can be the judge now, who do you think is doing the right thing between the man who marries openly, and the one hiding some of his wives?" Abuk asks, now turning on me as if to invite me into the talk. I think I have had enough.

"All of them are sinners and they must go to hell!" shouts Kiden. I wonder if this is what the Bible teaches about polygamists, both men and women.

CHAPTER 6

April 21st 1997, Khartoum, Sudan

"Is this the reason we still have both China and the US as our best friends besides Russia, Israel, and others?" I asked, with my face turned away from the old man as I still want to meditate more on my thoughts.

"The answer is yes, and no. Yes, because some of us today have misunderstood our hero's views and his personal vision for the country," he said.

"What was Garang's view or vision then?" I asked, looking back at his trembling hands as if to get a hold on them as we talk heart-to-heart about our country and its past and present history. Nhial knew my questions were out of curiosity for learning.

"His view was that Sudan must remain united. His vision was that the system of governance must change. He wanted our Arab brothers and sisters to make the country a democratic one. He wanted to end the dictatorship. He didn't want us to separate ourselves from the north, *yani, huwo kan ma deru al infasal kulu*," he went on to say the same things in Arabic as if he didn't make his points clear in the English language.

"Then whose vision was it for the separation of the south from the north?" I asked.

"Well, it was what the people of the south demanded for in many years, even during the times of the Anglo-Egyptian Sudan. As I said before, we don't share anything in common with the Arabs in the north. In fact, Nubians, Darfurians, and even the eastern Sudanese, are not Arab, and they don't have to, but they have to liberate themselves from the bondage. Yes, Anya-Nya II was the real separatist movement because it wanted to revive Anya-Nya I's vision, which was nothing less than separation," he explained.

"I see. But why was the Anya-Nya II fighting against the SPLA, if at all they wanted was that the south must officially separate from the north?" I asked, looking at the old man once again in the eyes as if I knew the answers to my own questions.

"Well, the Khartoum Agreement of 1997 was not signed by Anya-Nya. Rather, it was signed by many leaders from the south, representing their own groups. That means it was not Anya-Nya II that was even fighting against the SPLA by then, but many different groups who broke out from the movement because of its tribal leadership," he went on.

"Do you think the Khartoum Agreement led to the Comprehensive Agreement of 9th January 2005?" I asked. "Yes, it was, why not? This agreement is the backbone of the CPA because it paved the way for the peace and self-determination of the south. Dr. Riek of South Sudan Independence Movement (SSIM) headed the signing of it because the rest were not considered to be of any value apart from Kerubino who pretended to represent the SPLA, but he was not sent by them. The SPLA didn't want the separation of the south from the north. Rather, its leader was aiming to be the president of the whole old Sudan, which is why he later on missed it and died on the mountains instead. He didn't know that Arabs are not that easy to deal with. If you want to know about how evil they are, ask their brothers, the Israelites," he went on to explain.

"Apart from Dr. Riek of the SSIM and Kerubino Kuanyin Bol of the SPLM, who else signed the Khartoum Agreement?"

"Well, there was Aru of Union of Sudan African Parties (USAP), Ochang of Equatoria Defence Force (EDF), and Makwei of South Sudan Independents Group (SSIG). But as I said, those groups were not an issue to the Sudan government at the time. The SPLA and the SSIM were real threats, but the SPLM's real leader was not there to sign the agreement, and he didn't even send anyone to represent him. This led to the failure of the Khartoum Agreement, simply because Dr. John Garang of the SPM/A did not agree with this act," he explained.

"Does it mean that Dr. Riek Machar Teny is indeed the one who spearheaded the independence of South Sudan, and therefore the true founding father of the nation?"

"Well, before him were many others such as Samuel Gach Tut and others such as Jaden, a Madi rebel leader of the Anya-Nya I. These men had the vision for a separate state of South Sudan long before Dr. Riek came into play. Yes, it's a long story to be frank," he went on.

"Does it mean that even Dr. John Garang de Mabior was not the founding father of this nation?" I asked, looking at the old man in the eyes. He then smiled and looked away before he answered.

"Well, it seems you want me to get into trouble. But, I will always answer your questions from facts, not from my personal opinions, or even from my imaginations. If one becomes a founding father because of having the idea about the country, then it's true that he was not," he said, looking at me again.

"But why did they put his head on the money and preached to the people that he was indeed the founding father of the nation?"

"Well, we don't have to deny his work. He was indeed a person of his own abilities that none of the leaders before and after him did possess. They have a saying in our language that if you want to ask for a piece of meat you have to ask for the whole leg first so that the owner considers to give you a piece instead of the whole leg, and I think this was what many of us assumed. We think he asked for the whole Sudan so that if not possible then we will get a piece, and that's South Sudan," he went on to explain his riddle. It sounded familiar to me though.

"But, the Dinka are also evil, and that's why we say, "/ *Ca bor Jäŋä lak*," because you never know what they are up to at the moment. Whatever they tell you is not always correct because they have that natural inclination to deceive others in order to gain or win for their own interest," he said.

"I think all humans are like that, aren't they?"

"Well, they are, but these people differ a lot based on how they were brought up. Culture is still a great force as an influence in the human life. We are who we are because of both nature and nurture, young man," he explained.

"Yes, and that means all Dinkas are not the same, isn't it?" I asked.

"I mean, why do We had to generalize a certain tribe or group of people, if at all there are both good and evil folks everywhere?" I asked again.

"I am not imagining how evil these guys are. Rather, I know what I mean, young man. It's not an imagination but a fact based on the past experiences about how these people think, speak, and act. These are things that I have seen and heard!" he shouted.

"So you mean to say Dr. Garang did not want to sign the agreement because it will appear that if we gain our independence as a result, then our people will praise Dr. Riek instead of him?"

"Since he didn't want the idea of the separated federal south, he refused to sign the agreement. It was not because of whom to win the agreement, but it was all about what was outside his vision: New Sudan," he explained.

I was still thinking about the Dinka ideology. Indeed, there are internal wounds that can't be healed easily. We still hold grudges against each other as the people of South Sudan. I wonder when we are going to say enough is enough. I wonder when we are going to recognize ourselves as one people.

"I think Garang was just himself. He was not a Dinka, but Dr. John Garang de Mabior Atem. He had his own heart, mind, spirit, and soul. What do you think?"

"I think he had all those things in a Dinka way, and his actions revealed the truth about him," he said. This statement turns me off-road. Whenever I hear such comments about other people groups, especially from those who are the educated few, I develop some kinds of stomach aches. This is something personal. I don't think all humans must think or react in the same way to issues such as these. But this is always painful to be to be frank. Am I fearful in nature?

"Is there anything like a Dinka way?"

"You don't seem to understand. Maybe you won't. What I mean by the Dinka way is that these people will always try to cover up realities with lies as long as those lies serve their purposes. But for us, the Nuer, we speak the truth, no matter what."

"Are you telling me that all Nuer people think in the same way all the time? Don't we also have people who cover up lies?"

"In principle, I agree with your argument. But in reality, you're going to find out by yourself. These people are too clever. They'll make sure they will rule this country forever because they're naturally cunning evil. You may get annoyed with me, but who am I anyway? I am always a dead man though I live."

Oh, my God! This statement is made me sick. Indeed, he was a dead man. I can tell. But he was still alive and well. I can see, hear, and feel his presence. He was here with me though he was soon to be buried somewhere near his hut.

"I don't understand this. I think all humans are the same in some ways. They're but all human, aren't they? Generalizing either Nuer or Dinka is not right. It's another way of saying that we don't trust each other as people groups, here in South Sudan. I don't agree that all Dinka people think, speak, and act in the exact same way. In every tribe, there're both good and evil people, is this not so, grandpa?"

"You're free to think in your own ways. This is good. It means you are a human being, and you have your own beliefs regardless of what others believe in. But as I have already told you, take time to explore these sayings. I came to those conclusions over many years of research. Don't even think that research happens only in a confined classroom. It happens everywhere, and it happens all the time."

"But are we friends to the US?"

"We are. They helped us come out of the hell on earth, didn't they? Garang did his best to make them believe we're all Christians, but this is a white lie. Yet again, this trick served its purpose. We're now a country of our own. We also have a good friendship with both Russia and Israel, but I can't go into more details into this. Why do you want to know?"

"I want to know simply because it's good for me to know who are our friends and who are our enemies. In this world, you have both. You can even be your own friend or enemy, can't you? You think the Dinkas are always our enemies. I think that's too much. It's a generalisation. They're our brothers."

CHAPTER 7

August 9th 2019, Maaji

After leaving the Adjumani town, I and many others on board left for Maaji, a refugee camp located 24.2km west of the town. On that minibus were many other South Sudanese of different ages, genders, experiences, and qualifications.

"How far is it from here to Maaji?" I asked.

"Do you mean Maaji I, II, or Maaji III?" he asked.

"Oh, I don't know which one. Are they all located along the road? Which one is nearer?" I asked.

"Maaji I is nearer, then after it, comes Maaji III, and then Maaji II is a bit farther. We will go to all of them since I have got at least a person for each of these locations. Are you going to Maaji I?" he asked.

"No, I am going to Maaji II," I corrected.

We had to start on our journey, the last journey to the final destination. I wanted to see my wife, Nyaluak and our three children, Deng, Nyalang, and Chuol. I had to pay the fare, and there were no tickets or even receipts. The minibus was painted white, and it looked very much old that I stared at it several times before getting on board.

"Oh, okay, I can see that the signpost reads that the distance from here to Maaji is 24.2km," I exclaimed to the driver who has already taken his seat and ignited the old car, making that crazy sound. The exhaustive pipe seems as if it was facing the inside part of the car because the smoke was coming back in, almost making the driver to barely see anything on the road ahead of him. We in the car can't see each other properly.

"Look, Uganda, and South Sudan are almost the same in terms of development. Kenya is far ahead of these two countries. I wish I was born a Kenyan," said Juliet, a South Sudan woman, a refugee heading, who was to Maaji I.

"How can you say that? How can you compare South Sudan with Uganda? When did we get our independence? We have a long way to go to be compared to any of these neighbouring countries in terms of the infrastructure," Nyakong objected.

"At least we have peace so that we can travel to any part of the country even at night. But do you have peace in Sudan? Do you have roads?" asked the driver, whose name was Kaikara. He later told me that his name is a traditional name for God.

"You mean you don't know our nationalities? We are not Sudanese, we are South Sudanese instead," Amou questioned Kaikara the driver. I almost said something like that to the driver but as usual, she was twice faster than I could. That was another woman's ability I have seen that very day. Indeed, we are no longer Sudanese ever since the 9th July, 2011. This means Dr. John Garang was right when he said during the signing of the CPA that Sudan will never be the same again.

"You are but Sudanese. South and north are still parts of the same country. Why don't you want to be called Sudanese? You have to accept that you are a people from that country," Kaikara objected. I wanted to correct him, but I thought if he still didn't know the fact at that time, he was likely not to listen to me, no matter how I try to explain things.

"Please be quiet! The LRA are known to cross the road from here, each day. They are still hiding in the Ugandan bushes. They also go and steal food from South Sudan and Congo. They are indeed very merciless rebel insurgents in this world," said Tombe, the only South Sudanese male after me on board.

"Oh, you are afraid like a woman? I thought all men don't fear such things, what kind of man is this?" Nyabach, the woman seated just in front of me marbled and asks questions, looking at Tombe who was sitting on my left hand side on the minibus.

I felt bad about her comments. At least that was not a South Sudanese way for a woman to address a man she barely knows by name. But I had to remind myself that Africa is no longer the original continent it used to be many years back into our human history.

I wanted to ask her why she thought and spoke like that, but I couldn't. All of us on board, including our women, went silent for some minutes.

"You guys don't know how to fight. In your language, you used to say that you and the Arabs eat on the same plate/gourd. This means you are the best cowards in the land. You feared the Arabs and instead of fighting them, you gave them your girls for free. You even fought alongside them against the SPLA/M. What are you trying to say?" Nyakong narrated and questioned Nyabach, who was next to her. Both were seated behind me.

"Just stop it! Our bus almost ran into an ambush the day before yesterday between Juba and Nimule. These things are real, and you don't have to argue about it," I jumped in, mainly to silence the women.

"I think men are now afraid of death more than women do in South Sudan. Even a man with marks on his forehead can speak like this? I thought only men without marks are identical to women," Nyakong questioned and then answered herself.

Silence.

On our way, I could see large cotton farms with so many people working on them. I was told these workers were prisoners, but they are doing a great job for the economy of Uganda. Despite all the exports of cotton, banana, and coffee, the economy of

Uganda was not much improving. In fact, the South Sudanese Pound by then was ten times valuable than the Ugandan shilling. I began to think about what makes the economy strong. Is it about peace and local production? Is it political?

After an hour later, we all arrived to our various destinations. Some of us lighted the minibus at Maaji I, others at Maaji III, and finally, I made it to Maaji II. I was able to meet my wife, my children, and their neighbours, and relatives that very evening. It was indeed a blessed day.

However, I had no idea how life was in that green mountainous part of the world. The coldness, hunger, dreaded ghosts, and sickness were the inhabitants of this part of Uganda. I was about to experience them.

"When we came here in the early 2014, mysterious creatures used to visit us. They just disappear into the thin air whenever one has to look at them for long. We were placed in the bush. As you can see, there are tall trees everywhere. Water comes bubbling up from the ground. There are too many mosquitoes here, but you can't hear them sing," my wife narrated to me as we took our time, alone with each other.

"You mean you saw one of them? How does he or She looked like?" I asked. "Well, they looked and sounded like humans. They even spoke in our Nuer language, but when you try to go closer to them, they just disappear without walking away or running anywhere. They are but ghosts!" she explained.

"The food ration is not enough for a month. Five people in a ration card can receive less than a 50kgs bag of maize per month. Some people receive money. Five people can receive up to 150,000 UGX. This money is huge in number but less in value. We once ate wild plants that we don't even know if they are poisonous or not, but that was life," she went on.

"When you are sick, they don't treat you, especially if you visit the clinic in the evening hours, even if it is on the work day. Many people died at the clinic, just because the nurses and doctors neglect them and just leave them there to die. They rather sell you the best medicine in the shop, if you can afford it," she said with tears running down her both cheeks.

"The Madi people, the hosting community, hate us so much. They don't allow us to pick dried wood from the forest. They can beat, rape, and torture us. Even the piece of land we have around the house cannot produce well because they bewitched it. You men are enjoying life back home, but we and your children are here suffering," she speaks up as she sobs.

"I can tell you the fact that not all men are lucky. Some are dead and the living ones are suffering all kinds of pain. Do you think it's easy for me not to see you for years? Do You think I like it that way? But what can I do then? Our country is not yet stable. We have new rebel movements being formed almost every year. Is this a sign of peace? Do our people even love each other let alone our leaders?"

"You men only imagine how bad it is to be the only parent for your kids when your other partner is alive and well. Some of you end up getting married again back home and you keep reciting the same fake violence? How come that some men get married if at all there's no peace back home?"

"I am glad you said some. I know you know I am not one of those men. I can't get married when you're here suffering with our children. If I want to get married, you'll be the first person to know about it."

"I have no doubt about your love for me, Mut. But you men are always men. You never keep such promises. You'll one day get married again as you did before. I am not the only wife to you, am I? This also means you might be having one or two more unknown wives in South Sudan. But those unknown women become known one day just like the unknown gunmen on our roads. Nothing is hidden on earth."

"I understand your points and pain. It's bad. I wish our people come together and live in peace, but this is just a wishful thinking. Who wants to live in peace with those who have recently killed his people?

This is the situation we're in. Our people don't love each other. Even as I travelled, I've met both men and women who're so bitter against. I have no idea how long we will continue like this."

"Well, you can only imagine everything until it's time to die. But you're supposed to live your life to the full. Living life to the full means being worry-free. Think less about the current issues in the world. Don't put all that on your shoulders or else," She was spoken. At least, I can feel her conform. She was my dear wife. If all women think like this, the world would have been a better place. But they seem to do this to impress men. Before I made a mistake to get married to a second wife, all I used to hear from her was complaints. She ever been complaining about everything. But now, things look better because she always wants to help me, especially when she knows I am about to be depressed. Her love increased by fifty per cent because there's now a competition.

"I think I need those comforting words more than I need food and water. You're now speaking like a man with a womb. Does it mean hardships have now taught you to become wiser than a woman? Is living like a single mother teaching you something good in life? I am not saying this is good, but I am thinking."

CHAPTER 8

January 26th 1989, Nasir

"I was told that Nasir was captured from the Arabs and their toughest army, led by Mahajub, your nephew in 1988, but some said it was captured in 1989 instead, what do you say?" I asked.

"Nasir town was captured on the 26th January 1989, and there is no doubt about this historical fact. Anyone who was a grownup by then must know this. You were about 6 years old at the time, so you are right to ask. But that's my historical answer, as far as my mind could recall. Many others can confirm that this is historically accurate, if you ask them," he explained further.

"Who then captured it?"

"Well, there were many battalions in one unit. This makes it harder to say who captured the town from the enemy soldiers because there were many different divisions from different parts of the south," he said.

"But the SPLA captured the town from the enemy. It doesn't matter to me who to give the credit to because it was a victory for South Sudan," he explained his points.

"But in that year, things fell apart, right?"

"Yes, it was the same year when things were bad for the SPLA. The Ethiopian government was on the brink of collapsing, so was the government in Khartoum, Sudan. This was the year when Omar el Bashir took over the power. Many of our refugees from Ethiopia were forced to return home where the war still going on," he said.

"Who were the commanders in charge of the SPLA forces joining hands to capture Nasir on January 26th 1989?" I asked to help him return to the main topic of our discussion of the day.

"There were several of these SPLA commanders. In fact, the current president was there, comrade Salva Kiir. William Nyuon was there, Kerubino, Garang, Dr. Riek Machar, Dr. Lam Akol, and many others," he said.

"That was a large army. How many soldiers were there from the SPLA side?"

"Oh, I can't remember because I didn't actually know the number. A battalion is like a Roman legion. Who needed to know how many of them were there? The most important thing was that they managed to capture the town, and Mahajub himself, their brave commander, was captured alive," he said.

"Oh, okay, I see your point. Can you tell me a bit about this Mahajub? Was he tall, brown, short, black, huge, or thin? Was he bald-headed?"

"I think he was another man similar to the apostle Paul in the Bible. He was short, brown, and yes, he was also bald-headed. It seems you might have seen his pictures somewhere in the books, haven't you? How can you ask me about something you know? You have just described him in one of your sentences," he said before laughing out louder.

Nhial has a great sense of humour. He loves people. He loves children. He loves animals, too. His hut was full of dogs, and most of them were not his own. He's tall, brown, and beardless. Even though he seems to support polygamy, he has only but one wife, my grandmother, Nyanchar. She was indeed very dark, short, and strong. Her teeth are as white as snow.

My father is also tall, brown, and handsome. I and my other siblings resemble him. My mother is short and dark-skinned. She was about half of my father's height. But I am not medium as many may think.

Nhial is one of the elderly and well educated men of the nation as far as the education of the 1900s is concerned. The highest level of education by then was the elementary school, which was mostly provided by the Western missionaries. This is where my grandfather went to school. It is quite the opposite that my father didn't know how to write and read. This is partly because my grandfather fed up with the chaos in the country, and he then left the town only to live in the villages of the Upper Nile region where there was little to no schools. Nhial's education made him think the way he does. He is always objective in his thoughts instead of being subjective. He is a liberal thinker, a liberator, and a family man. Men of all ages loved to sit by him and listen to his tell-tales. He is a good storyteller. Of course, who in Africa is not a good storyteller?

"Do you know Mahajub in person?"

"Yes, I know him, and I think he can remember me, very well, unless he is mentally sick or old enough by now. These red (Arabs) and the white (English) people become old very quickly, but I am much older than him," he said.

"Are there no books written about him?"

"I have no idea if there are books about Mahajub and the other SAF commanders in the south during the war. But I think if I can search the wealth of the Internet, I may find something about them, including their pictures. But you are a book, aren't you?"

"Books don't talk! I am Nhial, not a book," he said and then smiled as usual. He loves jokes. He makes me laugh from time to time. We were friendly more than I and my father were. He was indeed a different human of his own. Despite living among the hostile people, my grandfather was far from it.

"Was you there when Mahajub was killed?"

"Yes, I was there, but he was captured, not killed. He was then taken back to his rightful country, his place of birth, and that is north, now called Sudan. I feel sorry that they now called us South Sudanese as if we are still part of that country. We are supposed to come up with a completely different name for this country for the world to know us better. Now, even our neighbours still call us Sudanese," he lamented.

"Then what happened to the rest of the soldiers captured together with him?"

"Some soldiers ran to the north. They thought they could make it by footing, but they then died of thirst in the bushes. Some were killed by angered fathers and brothers of the men and women they killed during the Nasir Battle. It was a disaster for the red folks in a foreign land. I think if you have to bring them back to life, they will curse their government," he explained.

"Does it mean everyone in the Sudanese armed forces must be red?" I asked, looking at him with a lot of seriousness in my eyes.

"No, not at all, my son. But most of their commanders and those of higher ranks were red. They were pure Arabs. Yet, the soldiers were the real Sudanese. Some of them were Nuer sons and daughters," he went on.

"Did they recruit and then send all these troops to the south from the north, or did they recruit some from here in the south?"

"Mostly, the recruitment into the Sudanese army was done far in the north. But some were recruited from here in southern Sudan. Some of our soldiers also sometimes defected to the Arabs, and they were added to their numbers," he said.

"Did you have any hope for the end of the war?"

"Yes, I did. I knew that the war will one day come to an end. Many people among us knew this, and that's why some told their younger brothers to put down their guns and go to the north for education. They knew that the war can also be fought in many different ways, including education," he said.

"How can education be another way of fighting?"

"Education is another way of fighting because one of the reasons why the Arabs marginalized us was because we were not educated like them. Education can open our eyes, so that we know our rights as citizens of the Sudan," he explained.

"Did you know we will fight our own wars?"

"By that time, yes, I knew because we have already begun to show signs of hatred among ourselves. The Nuer people were mistreated in Itang by the Dinka soldiers, resulting in anger on our side. Then we started attacking and killing innocent Dinkas when they tried to go back to Bahr el Ghazal, or Bilpam in Ethiopia for military training," he confessed.

"Were you one of those who killed these people?"

"When I say 'we,' I mean to say 'us,' the people. In our culture, if you happened to have done something, all of us are doing it. It doesn't mean I have killed anyone in cold blood, but our people have done this, anyway. They've killed innocent people, just because these were Dinka. This was a bad revenge on the wrong people. Those who mistreated our people were left behind in the military training camps.

"How do you feel about it?"

"When they killed those innocent children, and I heard about it, I felt terribly sad. We shouldn't have done this. And again, we the people shouldn't have done this in the name of tribe. I do believe that each human being will be judged according to his or her deeds. Killing harmless people is cowardice, and I can't entertain such a thing. In my culture, I was taught to face the person head-on, not from behind."

"After this historic battle at Nasir, I have heard many different stories. I was told that the Dinka people used to kill and eat the Arabs raw, right in the frontlines. What do you say about this? Is this a true story or is it another fiction just like those fictional stories of creation and the virgin birth in the Bible?"

"There're too many stories. Many people have chosen to believe in those stories regardless of if they were true or fiction. This is what the world wants to hear. In this modern world, truth is relative. Those biblical stories are fictional at best, and I am glad you know. I never seen it happening in frontlines, but I have heard of it. Even your uncle, Bangich Reat used to sing songs that seem to allude that some of the people he knew were almost eaten alive by the Dinka soldiers. What I know is that there are many wild animals in our area which feed on human flesh, even long before the Dinka people came to our land. For this reason, we can't tell who was the culprits, the Dinka or the wild animals."

"But do you believe Gatluak Manguel is a real person? I am sure you've heard many of his stories. I was told he even went to that side of Nasir up to the Gajaak areas where Kun Thoal made him pay heavily for trying to kill his people."

"Again, the stories are real even if the events weren't. I don't believe in such stories. This is fiction. A human may decide to feed on another human's dead body in some direst circumstances. This happened somewhere in the Bible, wasn't it?"

He's straightforward with his answers. I personally believe the reason why the Nuer don't want to associate much with the Dinkas is the concept that the Dinkas are human-eaters. Most of my people call themselves, Naath, which means human. Does it mean other tribes are not human?

CHAPTER 9

August 17th 2019, Maaji II

"I know the fact that you are traumatized, but I hope and pray that this becomes part of learning for you. Life is a challenge for all of us," I said to her, holding her with my left hand, just to make sure she was that much closer to my heart. I then kissed her on the forehead, relieving her worries for a season. At least, she was no longer lonely as she used to for the last five years of an unpredicted and an unplanned separation.

The first night was too short for us. We couldn't sleep at all. We talked heart-to-heart, moving back and forth into our very own history of marriage and relationship. We have been married for over a decade by then, and we never spent a year together ever since, all because of the war and the conflict back in South Sudan, our homeland.

The following day was a food distribution day. I had to go and witness how they receive their ration. My wife and I had to leave very early in the morning. Our children remained at home. On our way, we met many displaced people from our community.

After the food ration, I had to carry our bag on my shoulders, and my wife walked by my side like a queen, and yes, she was. But women of all ages began to criticize her for making me do this. Men were like golden vessels in the refugee camp, and one has to guard around her man whenever he happened to appear once after several years of separation, just like a full moon appears once in a month.

"It really looked odd for a man to carry a heavy load, why don't you help him?" said some of the women we met and then bypassed along the road back home. In this part of the country, you have to climb up and then come down as you walk the sloppy roads in the mountainous areas.

"She has been doing this for years, so I had to help because this is what marriage is all about," I responded to her critics before she had a chance to say a word. I could see she that loved it.

The following day, I found myself digging in her garden around the houses, which she built a few years ago. "Is that a Madi man?" asked a woman who was passing by. "No, I am not," I responded. This happened because Nuer men like me were nowhere to be seen in this village, which is filled up with mostly women and children. It was a different world with its own strange cultures and stories.

"Tomorrow morning, we will go to the market. I want to show you the kinds of things they sell here. Do you know about Ndeje? It's a Ugandan fish, the one similar to the ones we don't eat in our village in the Upper Nile. This fish is too small for adults to eat, but it is very delicious here. We are no longer human, I tell you," she said before smiling. My wife was now telling me stories about the camp.

On our way to the market, Nyaluak, my wife, could tell me more stories. They never come to an end. I had to learn the skills of attentive listening, which she believes is the first door to true wisdom.

"Many women here will grow old before they have as many children as they should. But some women already have children with our matured sons. Some women have children with the men from the hosting community. But not every woman can be able to share a bed with another man when she knows her husband is alive and well back at home," she told me.

"What if the husband is no more?" I asked.

"Well, it will also depend on who the woman is, based on her culture, as well as her personality. If she was born by her father and mother, she will have to wait like I did," she explained her points.

At the clinic, which was a few hundred metres away from my home, I could see with my optical eyes how both the host community and the refugees lost their loved ones to Malaria, a type I never seen before. People die, daily. Onc beautiful girl passed on in my presence even though I tried to pray for her. She was from Madi, the host community. One good and kind medical personnel on duty could do nothing. He referred her to Adjumani town, but the ambulance never arrived for the whole day to take her. The distance between Maaji II and the town was less than one hour by a Land Cruiser. But the vehicle failed to come on time. She died because her oxygen levels were getting very low according to Kennedy, a medical professional I found there.

"Can you now see the suffering of our people? Your son, Deng, almost died like that just the other day. I brought him here around 10a.m, but no one was on duty until 5p.m. The boy was very hot and he shivers. He was also vomiting until he was unconscious," she explained.

"Are these nurses and the other medical people qualified? Are they paid by the government of Uganda or by the UNHCR? Why are they treating the refugees in this way?" I could go on and on, asking such questions in my head, but who will answer?

On our way back home, we met two pregnant women, ridding on two different motorbikes.

"Do you see those women? Chances are they will all give birth by operation, not in the normal way. Almost three out of four women here give birth by the C-section," she went on. Tears almost fell off my eyes, but how can I do this when Nyaluak is looking up at me in the eyes? "If you men could see this and think like women, even just for seconds, you will stop fighting against each other for the sake of the presidential seat in Juba. You see, this war in South Sudan is meaningless. When we were fighting against the Arabs, it was a just war. But what are we fighting for right now?" she lectured.

I had nothing to say. I was shy and full of shame from the inside out. I knew she was right, but I was not in control to either start or stop the war back home. The situation is dire, but there was little to nothing to do about it.

The next day, I and my wife took a trip to the main market, where they sell this little fish of different sizes. Some were very small, and others were bigger. I also went to see drug shops where most of the health workers in the area sell good medicine to both the refugees and the host community members. At least, if one can afford, the better.

"These shoppers you are seeing here are only here for a few days, and then they will disappear only to come back a month later when the time comes for the food ration to be distributed. They come only when they know the refugees are receiving money and food rations," said Nyaluak.

I could see all kinds of things on both sides of the road. There were electronics such as solar panels, batteries, and torches. In this part of the world, solar power is a waste of money. It's rare to feel the heat from the sun, even at midday. A few men like me who once made it to the camp were always busy, playing different kinds of games under the trees in the refugee camp. They think they had no job to do apart from playing games, day and night. I had a different thought, and I usually think differently from the rest of the crowd.

"Look, our boys don't listen to us because they think they are men as young as fifteen. Our daughters get pregnant as early as possible. All this happens because you men are busy fighting a senseless war back home," she lamented as we sat in a shade under a tree of which I have no name for.

"I am glad you have come here, my brother. When you go back to your safe haven, you will know what I am talking about whenever I make a phone call. At least, you now know what is happening in this camp," she said, looking away from me. I could sense from the tone of her ever sweet voice that she was about to shed tears again.

I could only imagine how long it will take for South Sudan to become a real country, not a name. I could imagine how hard it is since all our young boys and girls in high schools in East Africa always think politics instead of their professions. Could all of them become government politicians in the future? My wife keeps asking the right questions. She was right. Always. But I don't forget the fact that she was enduring hardships, neither do I enjoy life without her. No man enjoys life minus his wife and children, at least that's not so to me. Maybe some men love it that way.

"Now you call me a brother?"

"What do you think you are to me? I am your sister. At least, I will die and still remain your wife forever, but will you? You already have another wife. Whenever you're with her, no calling, no memories of me. But I will always be with you, Mut. I will always think about you, no matter where I am. Even death will not do us depart as they say in churches today."

"You know what? I hate wedding at church because of that same thing. What on earth could people allow death to do them depart, if they love each other? Do people know what they're saying to each other? Those words are not even their own!"

"Well, I think it's also true that people still die whether they like it or not, don't they? This is what they mean when they say until death do us depart. They know death is not our role. We're not the factor. It comes to anyone, unannounced. Oh, if some people know when they're going to die, I don't know what they'll do to the others they hate."

"But I definitely don't want to tell you those things. I'll cry if I do this. I am too emotional when it comes to such family matters. Even though I am a polygamist, I love you in a very unique way. You're the only you. Your co-wife is not like you in any possible ways. You're special."

"Did you just say co-wives?"

"No, I said co-wife. You know you're two. I don't even think of getting married to another wife after this. It was a mistake, you know. Peer pressure is real. Just as you women talk yourself into divorce, men also talk themselves into remarriage. Polygamy has many causes to different men. Not all men want to be polygamists, I tell you."

"So, what was your reason to get married again?"

"I thought you knew."

"Tell me."

"Something was terribly missing, Mama Deng. I told you that you used to be different before my second marriage. I thought you were always the problem. Look, it used to take you hours to cook or wash a few clothes. Now, it takes you minutes, if not seconds to do it. I want to know why did you behave as you did."

"You still think I was the problem? I am sure you didn't get everything you were looking for in another woman, did you? We humans are different. None of us is pure. We come with our own unique issues."

CHAPTER 10

February 27th 1972, Addis Ababa

"I know that the Addis Ababa Agreement came as a way to stop the war, which was already going on. By this time, the South Sudan Liberation Movement (SSLM) was the leading political party, as well as an army on our side, and General Joseph Lagu was the leader of the movement. Now, what happened before the signing of this agreement?" I asked.

"Yes, you are right. Before General Lagu came into the leadership of the movement in 1971, there were several different independent commands. But he came to unite them into what was known as Southern Sudan Liberation Movement as you have said. This combined both the Anya Nya fighting units and the political party, the SSLM," he said.

"But why was there fighting in the first place?"

"Well, as we have said the other day, Sudan has been in two different sections since the Anglo-Egyptian rules from 1930-1956. This means the south is very different from the north," he said.

"Why is the south different from the north?"

"They are different. We are Africans, and they are Arabs!" he exclaimed. I could see some rage in him, either because I spoke as a child to him, or because of the wounds I was again scratching in his mind and heart. Indeed, these scars may still be bleeding from the inside of him. He has seen it all, first hand.

"What makes the south different from the north?"

"Well, they are Muslims, and we are Africans. We don't believe in either Islam, or its other version, called Christianity," he said. I couldn't get him right.

"Is Christianity another version of Islam?" I thought about it for a few seconds.

"I don't think all people living in the northern parts of the Sudan are Muslims. I know that in the south, some people are Muslims, others are Christians, and even many others are animists," I explained my views to the old man.

"Well, you are right. But we were neither Christians, nor Muslims before these imported religions, and their funny worldviews came. We believe God is both good and evil. He does all these because He is the only God. For us, we don't have any concepts of Satan, demons, or hell. I've told you before. But both Islam and its sister religion, Christianity, teach us these weird concepts today!" he yielded.

"So, the difference in religion was the cause of the deadly wars in the Sudan?" I asked.

"Yes, it was, and it is, and it is going to be one of the causes of war in each and every society, my son," he said. He's now looking away from me as a sign that he's still thinking deeply about something. Maybe he wants me to think deep as well?

"But that's not all. Resources, power, fame, and greed are parts of the whole. People want to benefit from the natural resources of the country, and the short way to do this is to be in the top government leadership," he went on.

"But I was told that the war in Sudan started right back in 1955, a year before Sudan as a country got her official independence from the Anglo-Egyptian condominium rule. What was the problem then, was it religion and resources?"

"Well, yes, it was both. The war started because the constitution of the day did not explain whether Sudan is going to be an Islamic state or a secular one. It didn't even make it clear if federalism is going to be the system for the whole country. They kept lying about the federal system, but didn't do anything about it, leading to the mutinies in the south. We in the south wanted federalism, so that we can govern ourselves," he explained.

"After the Addis Agreement, what happened?"

"Nimeiri, the president of the day, later on dishonoured the agreement by declaring the Islamic Sharia law, which was one of the very reasons for the war. He also declared Southern Sudan to be returned to its former three main regions. He said the agreement was neither the Qur'an, nor the Gospel," he explained. I just wondered what that phrase meant, but I guess it meant to say the agreement can be dishonoured or changed, while the other religious texts, which both Muslims and Christians believe in, cannot be changed or altered in any way intentional.

"Did you know that this will lead to war?"

"Yes, we knew that the decision by the then government was a clear indication that Sudan was going back to war, a serious one, and that happened later on in 1983, the year in which you were born," he explained.

"Your father then left his work in Khartoum where he served as a police officer for several years. He hated the Arabs ever since, and I think you have got that hatred from his genes," he resumed.

I could resonate with that. I don't just know the reason why I feel bad about the Arabs and the Arabic itself as a language. Maybe my grandpa is right. Maybe I just have those genes from dad?

But is it true that hatred can be passed down to children, especially when they are born at the time when you have such a feeling as a parent?

I know the fact that I might have also picked these thought patterns from the ether, or from others around me. Many people in my world think the same thoughts almost all the time, especially when there's a trigger. Denying this fact is just what it is, lying. But how long are we going to think like this?

"Do you think the Arabs have studied us?"

"Sure, they're our masters. They know us from the inside out. They knew what we were thinking long before we even rebelled against them. They also knew how they used to treat us with all hatred and contempt. But all of them are never the same. Mark that well. Not all the Arabs hated us that much. Yet, those on power always wanted to do away with us in the south."

"Was this the reason behind the hidden factory?"

"You mean the one bombed in Khartoum?"

"Yes."

"Yes, this was part of the long-term plans. They wanted to kill us with those nuclear weapons, but our friends saw it and bombed them. Our friends have the eyes of God. They even did the same thing to Iran, many years ago when France and Iran wanted to create the same thing to eventually destroy our friends. This is history, and you need to know about it. They always have evil plans against us."

"We have many friends."

"And I think you know who I was referring to, don't you? Israel! They're not just our friends. They're our biological brothers and sisters. We're Israelites by blood. I don't have a book about this to confirm the historical facts behind it, but my very own DNA testifies to this. You are an Israelite, too! This is why you naturally find yourself in that conflict in your heart with the Arabs. This evolutionary memory can't be lost!"

"Do you know about a man called Sadhguru?"

"No, I don't know him. Who is he?"

"He's a man from India. He seems to be in agreement with you when it comes to such things like memory. He teaches that we're a hip of food, energy, and memory. You are teaching me the same things right now, grandpa. Do you think God is the highest form of energy?"

"Before we go to those things such as God, are you satisfied with my answers to your other questions? I don't' know much about God. I don't even know if I want to know much about Him. But life itself is enough to teach us how to live our lives."

"No, I am not done yet. I still want to know why there was fighting before the signing of the peace agreement in Ethiopia in 1972."

"Good. Then let's talk about that. I had told you my part. I think the reason was that the government wanted to silence the guns, and it did, at least for a while. This was not the end of conflict. But long before this, there were just as there are some conflicts between tribes all over the country. Tribal hatred is not a new thing, my son. Even the Arabs in the far north had their own conflicts many years ago. They do have their smaller tribes, just as we do in the south. I just don't know why the south is always at war with the north almost in each country on earth."

"Sure, and I am about to ask you why."

"There you go. I don't want to lie that I know the answers to every question you might have. But what I know is that humans are naturally evil. This happens because of the accumulation of the wrong ideas about themselves. I remember you telling me how many of us believe that the Dinka people are human-eaters. Do you still remember that?"

"Yes, I do."

"Great. Humans are the cause of this evil. They're evil. They create conflicts. You as an individual, you have conflicts with yourself. But if you can just live your life as it is, you'll enjoy it. You'll have peace, the peace of mind, and this is life!"

"But how can I live in peace when my world is in pieces? For example, we don't have hospitals around. My mum died of an unknown illness several years in the village. She wasn't treated because we didn't have modern medicines. How can I then live in peace if life is but a mystery like it is?"

The old man is now looking at me in the eyes, saying nothing for some moments. I can't read his mind, no matter how I try. He seems to have a different way to express his thoughts apart from using words and facial expression.

"Don't you know that people still die after wasting a lot of resources for nothing? I am glad she died within the day she got sick. Do you know what it means when our people say we ate him or her after someone finally dies? It means they got tired of him or her because he or she was sick for a very long time. This is a burden. Let the dead rest in peace!"

"You mean I don't have to blame the Arab-led government on her death?"

"You don't have to. Many are alive today though they've gone through hell on earth. Do you have any idea of how my life was many years ago when I was a young man like you? It was horrible, my son. Imagine, we didn't have clothes. Coldness was our friend during the nights. Though we had plenty of free food to eat, things weren't pretty. Your world is much better than ours, yet you're complaining. Humans will always complain about life, yet they want to live. If you threaten to kill them, just to take pain away from them, they're likely to kill you first, if you're not careful. What do people need? Do they complain, so that we help them? No. Humans complain because they love complaining. It's their nature."

CHAPTER 11

August 17th 2019, Maaji III

"I know you haven't seen all of it yet. Let's go to Maaji III now, so that you see more of the hell on earth," she said.

"What is happening in that place? Do you mean something worse than what I have already seen here is still to come?" I asked, looking at her dark shinny lips. She still looked the way she was a decade ago before she mothered our three kids.

"If you can only stay here much longer, you will see it all. But I guess you are about to leave us. I wish I can tie myself around your wrest and then you carry me with you, but where can I leave my children?" she asked.

"Some men are really good and caring. Look at this man now; he's walking alongside his wife. We will die here before we see our husbands, or we just forget about them and instead use any man we can get," one of the three women seated under a tree spoke up as we passed by. She spoke in the Dinka language, and I guess she thought I didn't hear or understand what she said.

"Look, the Nuer men are wiser than ours. They at least come for a visit, but our men don't. I think this man came to see his wife. I know this woman. She has been coming here to buy things in the market. She was friendly and loving. Her husband must also be a good man," one of the women seated at the marketplace spoke up. She went silent when I turned my head to her direction and she decided to look away from us. Telepathy is a reality in all humans and animals. But that was not the case because this woman actually spoke up in Arabic.

Later on that very day, I decided to join the few men who were busy playing cards under the big trees, so that I could hear from them. Most of them were studying in the refugee camps.

In these camps, people are grouped by their tribe. You can find the Dinka people in a block or section of the camp, and the Nuer in the other separate block of the same camp. The UNHCR never mingled the people from South Sudan.

"The Nuer people and their leaders brought us to this land, which is good for us because without it, we can't learn how to read and write in the English language," Kaman, one of the men spoke.

"No, how can you say this? We never rebelled against anyone in South Sudan. The 2016 alleged coup was not even a coup in the first place unless one doesn't know what happened," Kang, one of the men playing cards objected. At least in this block, the Dinka men used to come in the evening hours each day to play cards with our Nuer men. They have known each other by name. They are good friends as far as they are not touching on anything political in nature. But how possible is it for the South Sudanese men not to talk about government politics?

"You better think about how the host community, together with those who came with us as refugees, are mistreating our people. They are the same people, anyway. The Madi of South Sudan and that of Uganda are but the same. They hate us so much," said Gatdet.

"They don't know the difference between a Nuer and a Dinka. After all, we have the same marks, which is why the regime in Juba killed some of our people, thinking they were Nuer. Did you know that many of our able young men died like that in Juba and in other places in South Sudan?" Miabek asked, while looking at the rest of the men seated under the tree as if to wait for their approval of his statement or its rejection or both.

"Last year, they killed their own person, and then dumped his body on the road near our block. But a few days later, the Ugandan police came to collect the body and they arrested those criminals in the next camp. I don't know how they were able to trace the killers," Mut, my name mate explained.

"Well, these people are educated. They either have satellite cameras, or they use a certain device to scan the eyes of the suspects. If you have killed someone, and you look into that thing, your picture appears in it and you are then arrested. That is how technology works, here in Uganda," Kon, a Dinka man explained.

"Actually, it is the other way round. They scanned the eyes of the dead person in order for them to see the killer in his or her eyes. The human eyes are capable of taking a picture of the killer and keep it there for some days, or ever forever. Maybe this is how God is going to judge us one day," Biliu, a Nuer man corrected him.

"How is the regime doing in Juba?" Kon asked me in the Arabic language.

"The regime is doing well. They have a business. They know exactly what they are doing," I explained.

"Oh, do they know what they are doing? That president of yours has nothing else on his head except that American cowboy hat. It was given to him in the US by George W. Bush because he knew this guy fits well to be taking care of the cows in his home. He is not and he will never be a president," Miading said.

"You Dinkas are very clever and cunning people on earth. If you can only give us a chance to rule this country for one year, you will see a tremendous change in all sectors," Mut said.

"No, that's not true! Nuers don't even have equality between men and women. Your women eat at last after you men have eaten, and in most cases, they sleep hungry, especially if there is a shortage of food. How can you pretend to lead a nation? You will loot everything in that one-year man!" Miabek explained.

"You are right, Mut. This man is mad, but it's not all Dinkas, its him and his group," Miading said.

"Because you say that there is no forgiveness between you and the Dinka, that's why you will never manage to get that seat, no matter what. If you rebelled against this weak and greedy government, you would have won a long time ago. Not all Dinka people taste the national cake, but when you go to war, you say you are fighting against the Dinka instead of the government, and that's your weakness," Miading went on.

"It is always the government that kills the innocent Nuer civilians just as it happened in December 2013. We only responded to that act of inhumane in Juba. This means it's not us who showed the world that the government and the Dinka are but the same entity. How can you say they are not the same if the Nuer people were hunted from door to door?" Mut asked.

By now the then good game playing turned into something different. These men began to speak as loud as they can. You can be able to hear them speak a mile away. As an introverted being, I began to feel the discomfort and I wanted to just walk away without saying goodbye. The same talk on the publish buses on the way to Uganda, and within our country, was right there in the refugee camps.

You can hear and see the results of war everywhere you find the South Sudanese. People speak words you can't believe they can speak to each other. It is very clear that the scars are indeed bleeding. The wounds of the past two civil wars in the Sudan are still yet to be fully healed.

Going back home after that evening meeting, I could see that my elder son had a bad leg.

"What happened to your leg, Chuol? I asked.

"Father, it was that tall, that huge Dinka boy. He stood on my way when I was going to school. He then started a fight with me for no apparent reason. I was alone, but I managed to later escape from his ugly hands," he explained.

"I was not there, father. If I was there, I would have killed him on the spot! He is truly our enemy, and I swear, I will find him one day," Deng, my five years old boy jumped in.

"Oh, my God! If little children like these could speak such words, when are we ending the conflict?"

"Who told you it's good to kill him?"

"But why did he hurt my elder brother? I don't have to wait for anyone's permission to fight for my rights. It's my right to live and be well, and so does my younger brother. Besides, these boys are bringing tribal hatred into the camp. This is not even our country, but they always cause chaos," Deng goes on.

"I just don't want you to say such things such as killing. Do you know what happens after you kill someone? You also run for your dear life. It's better said than done, my son. Don't let them teach you bad manners because you're not them and they're not you. Do you understand?"

Deng don't talk much. He sometimes seems as if he's not paying any attention to the speaker. He's listening and staring at me. You can hear the silence in the room. I don't know what's going on in his small head. Maybe he's in agreement?

"I understand, father. But do these boys understand anything. They always talk about the Nuer in a wrong way. They think we're the only glutton people on the face of the earth. They think everything Nuer is negative or evil. These are bad people!"

"Deng. This is what I meant when I said don't allow them to teach you their bad manners. Not all of these boys are evil, don't you see this fact?"

"Yes, father. I even have some of them as my best friends. One day, a Madi boy wanted to attack me, and one of my Dinka friends stood in my place. He fought to protect me from this fat boy!" Chuol says with giggles as if to remember the details. He seems to fully agree with my point. Not all Dinka or Nuer are bad people. In every tribe, in every clan, and in every family, there are both good and evil personalities.

"But don't you remember how they always want to tease you? They want you to get annoyed all the time. I don't know why they behave like this," Deng resumes, looking at his younger brother who is now seated next to him on his left hand side.

"Learn to love those who hate you."

"That's not possible, father."

"It's possible. It's only impossible if you think it's not possible. This is the teaching I want you to listen to. People are always who you see them to be. It takes time, but when you master this fact, it will work miracles for you."

"Do you think your son knows what a miracle is? He's a man of war, just like his grandfather. By the way, how is Nhial, your grandpa? Have you met him recently?" asks Nyaluak. "He's doing well, but very old. I don't even know if I will see him again. He's sickly nowadays. Old age has come on him like a thief in the night. But he's alive."

CHAPTER 12

September 10th 2019, OPM, Adjumani

It was a great time to chat with my kids in the small grass-thatched structure my wife built several years ago. But something disturbing started from the outside. It's a police car, a green-painted pickup truck with several police officers on board. The car hooting was so loud. I then came out to see it.

"You are under arrest!" shouted a man in the Ugandan police uniforms. And before I knew it, my hands were already clamped with a ring on my back. As I tried to fight, it was nonsense. I fell down face first on the rocky ground, and my legs were soon joined with a ring.

"Don't kill him! He's my husband, and he's very innocent. He just came from Juba to see us. We have been here for the last five years without seeing him. Please, I beg you, leave him alone!"

But all that shouting was like telling the brutal police officers to tighten the rings even more.

"Woman, get out of here! Do you know what this man is doing? He's a criminal, and he must face the law. This country is not like yours. It is governed by the law. He came to spy on the refugees and to collect data for unknown reasons. If he is a journalist, why didn't he tell the authorities about it?" the man questioned my desperate wife. But all was too late. I had to leave my family. They then threw me onto the military pickup car and the journey started. I had no time to even take my bags or clothes.

The one-hour drive to town was like 100 hours of pain and hurt. I had nobody to talk to. I sat on my back like a bag of maize. I can't get a hold on anything despite the rough road. But thank God, we made it to the town afterwards.

"Bring him here!" he shouted.

"Oh, young man. Where are you from? Can I have your passport?" he asked, looking at me right in the eyes.

"Here," I said.

"You people are so full of violent!" he shouted.

"What have I done really?" I asked.

"You have to tell me why you are here!" he blasted again. "I went to the refugee camp to see my family," I said. "Is it your family? What do you mean? Are you a refugee yourself?" he questioned, still looking at me in the eyes. I had no idea if these are his natural eyes or the substance has recreated them both in size and colour.

"I am not a refugee, but does it mean I can't see my wife and children who are refugees?" I asked. He then looked away from me for some seconds before trying to give me an answer, an excuse or both. It seemed he's thinking about how to answer me.

"Listen, you are not supposed to go the camp with your passport. You had to first take permission here from this office before you go there. You are charged of visiting the camp without taking permission from the authorities," he explained.

"I see. So what is the punishment for such a sin?"

"You have to bail yourself out or else we take will you to the prison so that you help us harvest the cotton. We have plenty of it and we don't have enough workers," he ridiculed.

I could remember how famous Jesus' stories are. The cotton harvest is indeed plentiful, but there are few workers on the fields.

"How much is it?"

"Well, you are now talking. Just pay 10m UGX in cash. And if you can pay it here right now you are ready to go."

"Will I go back to the camp?"

"If you want to go back to the camp, that will be your choice, but first bail yourself out. If you don't do so in the next 20 hours we will send you to the prison. You are a criminal, just like your so called leaders in Juba. They are here, playing sex every night, and your country is in pain. What kind of people are you?" he questioned. I could see anger as well as ridicule in his eyes. He meant his words and there was no single shadow of doubt about it. He needed clean money from a dirty country he rightly despises.

"But sir, I don't have money on me right now,"

"Then you will be in jail for life!" he shouted! I got then annoyed with his attitude. I suddenly forgot it's a foreign land where anything can happen.

"I told you I don't have the money. I also want to know if you will provide me with a receipt. If there is no receipt, then I am not going to pay criminal money. You better do whatever you want to do, right now, right here. I know your country is governed by the law and so is mine. Are you a lawyer or a police officer?" I questioned.

"I know how lawless you are. But you will not see the sun again! Nuers are forever rebels. Take him away from here!" he threatened. But I was as calm as I can. Two policemen on my right, one policewoman on my left, and they all moved towards me.

"Never touch me or you will regret!"

"Get him! Take him away from here!"

"I will not leave this place. Kill me or I kill you all. Tell me why you arrested me and brought me here. Is it that you come and ask me to pay you money? Is the government not able to pay your salary?" "I say take him!" he shouted. But the three officers were reluctant to his threats and orders. I was ready to attack in any possible ways, if they have to hit me or do anything harmful. They all had their AK47 riffles with them, but I was not alarmed. It seemed the officers were planning something.

"Are you sure you can fight all of us and win?" asked the policewoman on my left. "We don't want to hurt you. We want to take you away from him, just for a while. Would you come with me?" she said.

I looked at her beautiful female African face and she replied with a wider smile. Then she turned around as if to lead the way. I then turned towards her and she walked as I followed on her. I also kept an eye on the other two men behind.

A few meters away, we both walked into another door. The two men were still following. But before I knew it, she was on the other side of the fence with another door of which she opened and closed after her. The two men after me also closed the first door behind me and I was trapped. That compound was the prison. There were cells full of people.

I tried to fight my way through both doors but it was too late. It was getting dark in the evening. The vampire bats started to fly above in the sky. The nightfall has just begun. There was no chair or a tree in the compound. I had no one to talk to. I had to stand and wondered what the hell it was. Will they come back for me at night? Will they kill me or will they just beat me up? Whatever the outcome would be, I was more than ready for it. I was more than prepared. But my mind wandered. I went places from the inside until I almost forgot where I was present physically for about an hour.

But that dream world vanishes into thin air. It never meant to be there forever. It's always a temporary world of comfort, depending on which creatures and beasts live there.

I had to spend the night outside in the cold, standing, sitting, and lying down on the wet ground. In The next morning, the same policewoman came to take me away. I was placed in a car and rushed to the border. This time, I was free. I sat on the back seat comfortably all the way to Nimule, on the Ugandan site. There the officer and the driver told me to exit the country through the immigration office, which I did. All my legal and health documents were declared valid. Then they said goodbye to me as I walked through the small bridge into my country. I waved to them goodbye.

But I left all my belongings in the refugee camp, including my Smartphone, but my wife's phone number is forever saved in my internal memory. Soon, I had to let them know I was alive and well.

CHAPTER 13

March 6th 1993, Wijin, South Sudan

"Grandpa. Why was there fighting among South Sudanese in the villages, especially among those who speak in the same language?" I asked.

"What do you mean?" he asked.

"I mean, the fighting which broke out right in my presence in 1993 to present between the Lou Nuer and Nyikany Nuer of the eastern Nuer," I explained.

"Oh, yes, this fighting issue was there long before the independence of the Sudan. People have been fighting and killing each other for long. This is something about human nature. It is a serious wickedness, what do you think?" he asked.

"I thought you will say this came as a result of both Christianity and Islam, grandpa, why do you think it is about the human ego and wickedness?"

"Well, partly, it was a result of those two world views, but even long before these religions came, people were in war against each other," he explained.

"Does it mean humans, whether they are religious or not, are but sinners in nature?"

"Oh, yes, humans are wicked in nature, and wars can tell the story very well. People have been fighting against each other over simple issues in life, such as women, girls, cattle, natural resources, and much more, just to name but a few. They have been fighting even long people the Turkish people came into the Sudan," he said.

"You mean to say even the Nuer people have been fighting against each other long ago?"

"Yes, they have been fighting senseless wars and battles for centuries over the same issues I have mentioned to you earlier. There have been inter-tribal conflicts as well, and that was between the Nuer and other tribes around them, such as the Dinka and the Maban people," he went on.

"What was the root cause of the conflict between the Lou Nuer and the Jikany Nuer people?"

"It was a very simple thing, my son. It was an issue with a fish: lek. They then believed that the Prophet Ngundeng Bong prophesied this war long ago in the 1800s, when his fish, the same kind, was taken from him by force," he explained.

"Was it a curse from the prophet then?"

"They believe it was a curse from the prophet. But I think human ego is the main issue. A fish could not be the cause of such a big conflict," he said.

"What could be the remedy for such a disease?"

"Well, what do you think can be the remedy? Don't tell me it's Christianity or Islam, because all of these have failed and have contributed a lot to chaos in our communities. These are but other human interpretations of the world around them and its issues and situations. No human being knows exactly what the solution is for human ego and nature," he explained his points again.

"Well, I think in Africa, Christianity is not a mere philosophy but a life-changing force that can transform human nature into a new one, isn't it?"

"If you think so, yes, it is, but that's not always the case, my son. Human ego and human nature always rule over men and women regardless of their religious affiliations and confessions. They are still but real humans with real bodies and their own unique troubles, don't you know that?" he asked.

"In Africa, we were taught that smoking is a bad habit, so we don't smoke when we became Christians. Can that change be considered to be very important? Also, we were told it is evil to drink alcohol, and so many Christians today don't drink alcohol, is that not a transformation to be noticed?" I asked.

"Well, if they don't steal both substances, then that will be considered a good personality. But are you sure everyone will adhere to such commandments in Africa?" he asked.

"I think without Christianity I can't be the person I am today. This means to me that Christianity is a life-changing force because of the Holy Spirit, who is always at work in them who believe in Jesus Christ as their Lord and Saviour. This is a personal testimony. It is not wishful thinking," I explained.

"Well, then that's good for you, my son. But since I knew you long before you even know yourself, I know this is a misleading concept for you. You are who you are naturally, not because of Christianity. You see, those who believe are naturally believers. You can preach to all people but not all of them will believe you. If this is true, why is it so?" he asked.

"This is because they are wired that way, naturally. Even the apostle Paul was already a believer, long before he became a Christian. In the same way, there are both good and evil people in every society," he went on.

"Are you saying there is no need for Christianity and Islam in this country?"

"Yes, and also, no. Yes, because they both don't fix or change anything. No, because they are not a factor in our lives at all. It's up to an individual to become whatever they want to become, but that's none of my business to tell you to become who you are not, naturally. As I said, you are who you are by nature, not by nurture," he said.

I just wondered if I got these genes from grandpa, or if his life affected my thoughts and reasoning. I sometimes agree with him in some issues such as these ideas about personality. Are we who we are, naturally? Are we who we are as a result of nurture or upbringing? Are we who we are today because of both nature and nurture? These are questions to ponder a bit. I may think about them for life.

"Do you think we can change lives without Christianity or Islam?"

"Yes, but it also depends on what you mean by the word 'change,' in this context. What change are you talking about at the moment? Is it a change in the worldview or in the actual lifestyle of a person?" he asked.

"I mean the change in the whole of a personality, such as thoughts, words, and deeds," I answered.

"Well, people are who they are, naturally. The way they think is affected by their nature, not by what they learned from the outside world. If for example, you are a jealous person, you don't have to live with jealous people first in order for you to become jealous. You have it in your genes and you just act it out," he explained his points again.

"So what can we do to stop humans from fighting and killing themselves in our country?" I asked.

"Well, this is one of the difficult questions because I just don't know if anyone can be able to answer it. With our human nature, we can't live in peace with anyone. Even the apostle Paul knew this when he said somewhere in his writings that We had to try hard to live in peace with everyone. There are peaceful people in every society. But don't forget that there are violent people everywhere, and they will always outnumber the peaceful guys," he explained.

"Even your very own children will never be the same, my son. They will always be different. You will love those who are almost your type, but not those in the opposite direction, and that is also natural," he resumed.

"Do you have children who are violent?"

"Yes, even your father is such a violent child, and I think you know this, don't you? How many times did he beat you up each week for doing or not doing something right? Whether you did something or you didn't do it, he beats you up, right?" he asked.

Yes, I could recall how dad was such a violent man. I remember how I sometimes jump in between dad and mom to stop a fight even when I was a kid. I hate quarrel and fighting. I wonder if my grandpa passed on his nature to me, his grandson.

I hate to hear something about the fate of humanity. It sounds hopeless to a hopeful person like me. But it is a reality. Humans are both evil and good. Even the newest religion of the world seems hopeless at best. Religion doesn't transform people's lives as it promises. It's a mere hope or false hope. Humans are very happy at some point only to be very sad at the other turn. Life seems to have twists and turns, and some people think it's those who don't believe in God that face it rough in life.

"What about those who don't believe in a God? Are they not peaceful than those who believe?"

"It depends on what you mean by those who believe and those who don't. I don't think there's anything like not believing in a God. Those who claim they don't believe in God are lying or making stories. Don't believe them. They're doing some kind of research and they know that the best way to get answers to tough questions is to provoke you."

"But even the Bible teaches that there're people who don't believe in God. It calls them fools, right?"

"Yes, the fool says in his heart, 'there's no God,' and this is a true saying. Only a fool can say this. But most of the people who say these very things are not fools. They just want to play with your mind. They know the truth because they themselves are the evidence of God's existence."

"Are they looking for peace as well?"

"You mean those who call themselves atheists?"

"Yes. Do they think if we get rid of all religions, and their religious beliefs and systems we can be able to live in peace, here on the planet?" I am asking while looking at the old man right in the eyes. He then looked away from me, not because he's disappointed or shy but as his way of thinking of the right answers before jumping in, full force. He's wise.

"Well, not all of them think in the same manner. Some think in this way, but others don't. Some of the atheists are the most peaceful people on the planet. But don't forget that they're also human. Other atheists are the most violent people, too. This is natural. Humans are either naturally violent, or peaceful, regardless of what they believe in or not."

"Is the number of the violent people the same with that of the peaceful on the planet?"

"I think more people are violently wild in nature more than those who are naturally peaceful. Whether humans are rich or poor, their sinful nature causes them to commit sin and other serious crimes that come with it as a package."

"Can violent people become peaceful?"

"At least for a while. Violent people are what they are, naturally. You can't change either their thoughts nor their words or deeds. You don't have to change them. God made them that way for His own reasons. There seems to be a balance though in this creation. Look, do you love all insects? Do you know that we need all kinds of worms and all microbes in order for us humans to live? Everything is meaningful."

CHAPTER 14

September 16th 2019, Nimule

On the South Sudanese side, the officer in charge that day stamped my visa with an entry stamp, and I was ready to walk into the town to find a bus to take me back to Juba.

"How is the condition of the road now from here to Juba?" I asked the bus driver. He then looked at me before he said anything.

"Well, the road is good. It is tarmac. It takes about three hours now to arrive to Juba," he said.

"No, I meant to ask about the security."

"Oh, the road is not secure, but we travel by the grace of Allah. Do you get scared? Christians are not supposed to be afraid of death. Rather, they are supposed to have faith in God, right?" he asked.

I know about all those concepts, but since I almost had an accident on the same road some time ago, I still recall the fear and the anger I had at that time. His talk was like a joke to me. You don't joke with pain and death, do you?

But I realized that Muslims are not or might not be afraid of death. Could this be the reason why they can die because of their faith? Is this the reason why they blow themselves up in the name of Allah, the Most Merciful, the Most Gracious? I just don't know if my internal questions could get the right answers or not. I don't even know if they could get any answers, whether right or wrong.

It's still early in the morning so We had to wait for other passengers to come before we leave the bus station for Juba. The driver was asking me to take tea and some rest in the nearby teashop, a restaurant by the roadside, filled with other drinks as well.

"Come, it's time to leave!" he shouts. I had to sip my hot red tea faster. I had already got my ticket long before the other passengers came. I was the early bird. I always loved it to be on time. On board, we had several people from different nationalities and countries. As we entered the bus, I realized there were Sudanese, South Sudanese, Ethiopians, Kenyans, Congolese, Ugandans, Chinese, and other nationalities from other parts of the world. We then left the bus station at around 10:30a.m.

"Look, the Chinese people love our country! They even risk traveling with us on the roads. Why are they not using the plane from Entebbe to Juba?" asked Juma, one of the men on board, looking at me in the eyes.

"They are here because of their own interests, not because they love the country. You see, they always dig the oil out in any careless way because they don't care about the damage it will cause to the land, plants, animals, birds, and the human beings, living there. By the way, it is not their land in the first place, what do you think?" Nyuon, one of the male passengers seated in front of me jumped in before I could answer. But the question is not directed to me but to everyone on board who at least understands English.

"Tāmen zài shuō shénme?" asked Wang Yong, while turning to his friend next to him. He was one of the two Chinese people on board, who doesn't know English well.

"Tāmen zài tánlùn wǒmen," Chenguang answered. I thought she was saying, 'they are talking about women,' or something like that, but I had no clue at all. All I knew was that they both knew that we are talking about them in a negative way.

"Don't blame the Chinese or Ugandans for that matter. We have failed our country, ourselves. I wish Dr. Garang is alive. We can't be in the way we are now, if he is here, alive. There must be a law that governs everything," Yien, one of the male passengers spoke up.

"Oh, he was a bad man! Garang was not good. He was good, just for the liberation struggle, but he can't be a good leader for a nation. Did you know all he did in the bush? He was every evil!" Koang, one of the male passengers roared. "What is it about the Ugandans?" asked Adroa, a Ugandan citizen on board, a businessman who sells books and booklets in Juba, traveling to see how his business is doing over there.

"You have taken every job in Juba from building houses to selling water and clothes, leaving the nationals to go hungry. This is a bad attitude walai," said Nyawal, one of the female passengers on board. Wang finally began to smile and then he looked at me in the eyes. He sat on my right hand side, and his friend, Chenguang was on the far right at the bus window. I looked at Wang as if to ask him why he was smiling, but I didn't say a word.

"Why are you not talking?" he asked.

"I am silent because I don't know what to say!"

"Really, I thought every South Sudanese knows what to say about anything, but they have no idea of what to do about almost everything," he said.

"Oh, this Chinese knows how to speak in English so well! Why do you allow us to talk bad things about you and you are keeping quiet?" Ojulu asked.

"We are actually talking to each other here only that you don't understand Chinese. She was asking me about what you are talking about, and I told her that you are talking about us," Wang responded. And then silence sneaked into the bus for about ten more minutes or more before anyone could say a word or two thereafter. I guess we were reflecting on different things at the same time. Each one of us might have been thinking of something much more important. It was such a time when my grandmother, Nyanchar would say something like, 'the gods are passing by,' causing humans to be silent, or that one of the gods left us to watch over the door of his house for that moment of time. I have no idea if these concepts are real, but they send a message to us, don't they? Whenever you are silent, remember the myth: 'you're watching the door, or the gods are passing by.'

And suddenly, the gunfire echoed from the deep forest of the Equatorial region, then the bullets were punching through the metallic parts of the bus, and the driver lost control of the steering wheel! Wailing and fear was racing through us all.

"Get out! Get out of this bus!" the man in the military uniform similar to that of the SSPDF was shouting at the driver, dragging him down from the nose of the crippled bus.

"Can we hide? But where?" I asked myself.

"Come out all of you!" the man commanded.

I can't remember how I left the bus.

"Where are you coming from, and where are you going?" he asked. The man looked as if he was drunk. Indeed, he was drunk of something. He was one of the killers on the national roads, doing revenge on the innocent poor civilians who have from little to nothing to do with the government of the Republic apart from being mere citizens of such a beautiful country.

"Give me your documents!" he demanded. I then handed him both my passport and my national ID, also called the NC for National Certificate. Pulling all of them out, he then looked at me in the eyes as if to confirm I own the documents which were now in his hands. I looked at him in the eyes, there was no fear left when the worse comes to worse.

"You are one of the government officials and you are using this bad road? They use planes instead. Why are you using the road, huh?" he asked, pushing me on my face with his fingers to provoke me into a rage.

"I am a teacher. I love teaching children because they are the future of this great country," I said, almost under my voice. Fear is a real thing.

"Shut up! Do you have a country? Is this a country? You are eating all the oil money and you think you have a country?" he asked so fast that there was no time for me to answer him. But was he asking for the answers or was he asking himself? I don't know the answer to this question either. And suddenly, a military pickup came down roaring and rushing towards us as if it was on a mission to safe us all. The gunmen had no option but to flee into the bushes nearby. They suddenly disappeared into the forest. And then the feeling of relief came back. We could now see each other again. We were almost blind for those few minutes when the men held guns by our sides, pointing them at us as if to shoot and kill. We were like criminals caught on crime scenes. But the new pickup carries soldiers that wore the same uniforms looking like the ones those gunmen were wearing, and that could bring in confusion. 'Why are they running away from their own group?' That was the question in my head.

"You're lucky! They almost kill you all. This is the most dangerous spot on this road," said a captain after jumping off their military pickup and walking towards our bus on the roadside. The Chinese friends were shaking their heads endlessly in a surprising manner mixes with fear and joy for their own safely. We then knew that these were members of the South Sudan People's Defence Forces (SSPDF), the former Sudan People's Liberation Army (SPLA). But they looked like the gunmen who just ran into the bushes.

"You, come here! Are you now one of them?"

"No, I am one of the passengers, sir!" I shouted.

"But you are a rebel too, aren't you?"

"No, I am a teacher, sir!"

"You must speak well!"

"Please ask the other passengers. I came with them right from Nimule. I went from here to a refugee camp in Uganda to see my family because I have been in Juba for the last six years without seeing them since the war broke out. I am not a rebel, please! I am a South Sudanese. This is my country!" I lamented.

"You see? I know only rebels run to the camps, thinking those are their save havens. But now we have found you. You must speak well!" he said.

"Please, he is not a rebel!" Yien shouted.

"What? Bring the two of them on board!" he commanded. He then walked away while his men do his job for him. They blindfold the two of us and then tie our legs and hands and threw us into the pickup as if we were things. I then remembered what the leader of many soldiers who needed healing for one of his servants said in the Bible. He said he had many servants that he can say to this, "Do this!" and he will do it, and say to the other, "Go!" and he will go. We then left the bus on the road to proceed to Juba, but we headed back to Nimule as criminals, me, and Yien, my new friend. This was similar to what I faced two days back in a foreign land. Even though the road was tarmac, we were lying on our backs and some of the soldiers rested their legs on us as if we were sacks of sorghum or millet.

CHAPTER 15

February 12th 1998, Nasir

"I know what happened in Nasir back in 1998, but what was the cause of that death? Several government officials died there at the plane crash. I was there in person when the plane came down, but I don't know what caused the crash because the government never wanted to talk about it. I have many conflicting stories about this as well, but I can't judge which one is correct and which one is not. Can you explain what happened exactly?" I asked.

"Well, several things happened. But the main thing is that there was a plan to get rid of one of the officials on board by the then government. They wanted him dead for some political reasons, and he died!"

"Who were the people on board?"

"They were 57 people to be exact. I heard that 26 of them drown in the river. I recall Timothy Tutlam, Musa Sayed, Mohamed Kheir, Zubair Salih, Arok Thon Arok, and many other government officials and some military leaders were there. Some died and some survived the crash. Not everyone dies at the same time," he said followed by a deep sigh. "Do you think the government of Sudan by then planned their death because they were mostly South Sudanese?"

"No, I don't think they wanted them to die simply because they were South Sudanese, but because of some political issues. Politics has no relatives or friends. In government politics, we can be enemies today and become friends in the coming day. It's a place where truth as you may call it is far from the heart, but very near and close to the lips of every government politician," he went on.

"Is that not just another generalization?"

"Well, it's not a generalization. Rather, it's a matter of fact. This is what happens in the real world. Did you know that even Dr. Garang and Omar Bashir could eat on the same dish while the fighting continues in other parts of the country? They have no personal problems between them as leaders but political huddles. They don't hate each other in any way that you can even imagine," he said.

"Does this mean if I want to be a government politician, then I must be a liar?"

"Most probably, yes, you must be a liar in some ways. But that's my view. I know that truth is not in our government politics in South Sudan."

"What about in Africa, do politicians lie in order for them to get what they want from the people?"

"Yes, it is not only happening in Sudan or South Sudan. It is happening everywhere in Africa as a continent. It's the same thing in Europe, USA, Canada, UK, and in other parts of the world."

"Hush! Then I won't be a government politician if that's the case because many will hate me for telling the truth all the time. Or some will see me as a dump fool. This is because I will always try to tell the truth, or just my version of the truth. This will surely cause me trouble with others in the government, I guess."

"Yep! If you don't want to get into trouble, never desire to become a government official. But you will still get into trouble in life, won't you?" he asked.

I think he's right. Life has troubles everywhere, not only on one side of it. There are issues when people get married, and there is also enough trouble even when they don't.

"Why were there so many militia groups in the south in those days?" I asked.

"This happened because of many different reasons. One reason was that those who did not want to be reintegrated into the SPLA had no place to go, and they were already soldiers. They can't fit into the normal society. The second reason I guess would have been something to do with personal interests, or situations. People might have their own personal reasons why they became militias," he explained.

"You mean to say those from Anya-Nya II?" I asked. "Yes, definitely, I meant to say those veterans who were in the Anya-Nya II because they refused to join the Dinka-dominated movement. They had no choice but to join the government, or stay at home, if possible. But in those days, it was not possible to stay at home as a grownup man, because either the rebels or the government would come for you and take you away by force whether you like it or not," he went on to explain.

I do understand how I and many others were arrested in October 2000, just to for them to recruit us into an army we didn't quite understand by then.

"How many militias were there?"

"You mean all over the country, or on the side of the government? Well, on the government side, there were several, but the main one was what they called Dufashabi, which means the civil defence forces. On the rebel's side, there was SPLA-United, and several other small armed groups," he explained, looking away from the scene as if he was shying away a bit.

"Which civilians were they defending and from whom they defended them? Was it not the very same government who dropped those bombs on us?"

"They wanted to defend the people of the Sudan, including those of you in the south. It was indeed a Sudanese militia group, and you know that by that time Sudan was still one big country in Africa, don't you know?" he asked. "Yes, I know very well. But the reason why I am asking is that the government of the day was not a government for the whole country. It was a government for one side of the same country, Northern Sudan. Yet, as you can say, they recruited our sons and daughters from the south, so that we could fight against each other. But were these soldiers meant to protect our people in the south?"

"I have already said that they were pretending to do so, my son. But as you might have known by heart, what the government was thinking and planning was very different from what they did, and this is for a reason, a good reason. The Dufashabi was only meant to kill, rape, and to destroy people's lives and properties in the south. They were given salaries by the then government of the country, not to protect the civilians as their name suggests, but to be their agents in order to locate and fight against their own brothers and sisters in the nearby bushes. Have you not heard of these soldiers killing their brothers who used to sneak into towns at night to look for girls or visit their relatives, wives and children? It was terrible. It was horrible. It was bad, but it is now history."

"Indeed, grandfather, life is history in the making. This is one main reason why I feel at peace almost all the time because I know that my life too is history in the making. What do you think? Are we both not here to make history, each and every day, grandpa? I just don't like the fact that history always seems to be repeating itself. We are doing almost the exact same things today just as the Arabs did them to us when we were their slaves. Do you think life will change for the better? Do you think good history will come?"

"Indeed, we are making history, and I am afraid it's a bad one. We used to blame the Arabs but now where are they? Well, our people still give those who were with the Arabs the upper hand even in the government offices in our new nation. This makes me feel very sorry. Look, most of us who survived death are better to have died at the hands of the enemy in those days because we are not better in any way. We are still suffering in our own hands. What have we done wrong? Some of us were shot but was it because of their own cause or was it for that of a country?"

"I think they were shot for the freedom of men and women in this country, but people are people, grandpa. Do we even know what the government is trying to do right now? Do we know how difficult it might be for them to do that which we think they should be doing? I think there is something we are missing. There is something that we don't know as normal citizens of this country, what do you think?"

"I don't think we are missing anything. The only problem we have as people is that we don't accept each other. There is nothing like a tribal country, at least, I never seen one. But son, this is not a new thing. Even the Sudan you know was like this. Do you know that there are many different tribes even in the north, which is now called Sudan? Do you know that these tribes have been fighting against each other based on their ethnic diversities? It is not a new thing. When a country comes to her independence, many such things happen. I still hope and pray that there will be peace and stability in your country, even long after my death. At least, I have done my part!"

"Back to the event in the Nasir village, what can we learn from that event?

"Well, we can learn a lot of things about both the Arabs, and the people of this country. I can tell you that the Arabs were our masters, and not only that, they knew us from the inside-out. This is the reason they wanted us to vote for our own independence because they knew we are not going to rule or lead ourselves, at least for a long time. They knew we are going to divide ourselves along tribal lines, simply because this was what happened to them when the Anglo-Egyptian handed over to them their country through their independence on the 1st January 1956."

"What do you mean by saying tribal lines?"

"I thought you know the answer, don't you? By tribal lines I mean to say that we will not have any government in the real sense of the term, simply because we will not listen or obey our own government. Look, if your relative, who is a civilian, with a gun happens to kill a government soldier for whatever reasons, and then the killer comes to hide in your house, do you think you can tell the government about his whereabouts? No, you won't, especially if the soldier killed was from another ethnic group, and not from your own tribe. In this way, the government, too is likely to respond by firing at any civilian they see because they will think all of them are but rebels. If things happen in this way, where is the government? What is the difference between the government and the civilians? If the government is not capable of protecting her citizens, do you think the citizens will hand over their guns to such a government?" he asked.

"No, I don't think they will hand over their guns, and this is already happening right now. Even our soldiers still think along tribal lines. But I wonder if this is the case in our neighbouring countries such as Kenya. Do they still think along tribal lines today?" he went on. "It is hard to eradicate this mentality in Africa, my grandson. But if you keep thinking about it, each day, you will go insane!" he warned.

CHAPTER 16

September 16th 2019, Nimule

"Bring them down!" he commanded.

The men dragged us both out of the military pickup as if we were bags of maize flour or of Janjara. They then threw us down carelessly as if we were not human beings with flesh and blood just as they were.

"Untie them!" he shouted again.

Then they cut the ropes on our legs, leaving only the ones that were binding our hands backwards. I didn't feel anything. My hands seemed as if they were cut off, but I could see that they were still there. The ropes have entered deeper into my skin. I can't imagine being treated like this in my own country.

"What's your name?" he asked.

"My name is Yien," my friend answered between screams due to his painful hands, which were tied behind his back as if he was a soldier behind punished for his mistakes. I can recall when I was in a military camp back in 1998. Maybe I was much better than him because that training might have prepared me for this brutality. He also looked much younger than me. He might have been my firstborn son so to speak.

"And you, what is your name?" he asked, turning to me in the row. He looked at me right in the eyes, and I do the same. At least, this was no longer a foreign land for me. He can do whatever he wishes, but I felt at home at last. I can even tell which parts of the country he came from due to many physical signs and also his accent.

"I think I gave you my passport before. Check it and see my name on it," I reminded him.

The man was indeed a beast. He wasn't a normal human being. He could light three pieces of cigarette within about 10-15 minutes, almost lighting the next with the previous one. He smoked like chimney and drunk like fish. This reminded me of a movie I once watched about Nigerian pilot, who was deeply depressed because of his ex-girlfriend, and he then turned into drinking, smoking, and other drugs. Then his former pilot-friend told him that he smoked like chimney and drinks like fish.

"The guy is indeed a rebel! We must show him what it means to rebel against the government of the republic. Beat him up!" he shouts at his men.

"Sir, maybe you are a rebel. I can't be a rebel, no matter how you try to tell me that I am. How do you know that I am a rebel? Do you think all Nuer sons and daughters must be rebels? How can you say I am a rebel without any evidence?" questions just slipped out of my heart, and then out of my mouth.

"Shut up! How dare you speak to me like this? Take him there and give him some slashes on his foolish buttocks and bring him back here. Maybe he'll learn his lesson once again!" he shouted.

Before I knew it, I got something between a slap and a punch on my face. One strong young man had my legs and the other one took my tied hands with the ropes, leaving my body to float in the air for kicks and blows. I had no choice but to wail like an infant, crying for the precious milk of her dear mother.

Then the men laid me down and whipped my back and buttocks a countless time until their hands hurt them. They beat me up as one beats grain out of the husks, or as one beats a bird that can't be eaten.

"Bring him here!" he roared.

Then the men picked my body up and threw it in front of him. He then looked down at me, but I couldn't see him well. I was very dizzy and confused because of the blows on my kidneys. I was dying, and I could tell. I could only see dimly and barely hear voices, but can't move or say a word. My tongue was getting into my airways.

"Bring water! The rebel is now facing it rough," he mocked.

"Pour it on him. He's enjoying his slashes now. Ngɔth! Abä nyin thiɛth e cuɛ̈t, Nuɛ̈r!" he shouted at me in his own mother tongue.

"Yɛn cie Nuɛ̈r," I whispered.

"Hɛ̈ɛ̈! Yïn cie Nuɛ̈r?" he asked.

"Yes, I am not Nuer. I am a pure Dinka from Dinka Ngok Lual Yak. You have killed me for nothing, if you thought I am Nuer. I am a normal citizen of South Sudan. I will never rebel against my government, no matter what," I went on. He then looked at me when I was helplessly lying down on the rough ground on my bare back. I don't know what came to his mind when I spoke with him very clearly in his mother's tongue, or is it his father's tongue? He then switched between me and his men, speechless.

"You people resemble Nuer almost hundred per cent! Look at him. Can any of you tell me that he is not Nuer right now?" he asked.

"Look at everything from his posture, clothes, and those scarification marks, and his four removed teeth. This man must be Nuer. He's a rebel of Riek Machar. But we will show him what it means to be a rebel. Untie him and take him to Juba!" he commanded.

Then we left Nimule again for Juba on the same day. We had to travel at night. Thoughts of rebel attack were then racing in my head or heart as the lightest military pickup raced on the only tarmac road to the East Africa on its way to Juba. This was called, Juba-Nimule Highway as they used to call it when this was the only highway connecting South Sudan and Uganda. Silence ruled the car and the journey itself. Not only were the two of us silent but everyone on board was quiet and seemed to have been in his own world. The military pickup ran with its last speed set. The wind itself from the outside could slap you away, if you don't hold yourself properly. I can imagine if any slight mistake could occur, none of us would have made it for the crash would have been devastating.

"Are you okay?" I had to break the silence.

"Not very well, brother. I am in pain still, but at least, it's not like before," Yien was speaking under his voice as if to hide something. He had all the reasons to do so and I knew too well. The only truth now was that no matter if we were speaking anything or not, we were rebels. Our natural identity, or rather, the man-made identity, made us enemies to our very own brothers.

They might have thought we were their enemies, but I think this is wrong. I don't think all soldiers in the government, whether from Dinka, Bari, Shilluk, Maban, or Nuer, think in the same ways either. I think they were my brothers, but did they know this?

"We're going to be alright! This is not a new thing for me. I have been in and out of such situations as this, and I am perfectly alive and well. It might be your first time, but don't think about it too much," I advised. But I was not very sure if he could hear me speak due to the strong winds coming through even though I tried to increase my voice to give him a chance. I knew he was not sleeping. I knew he can hear me, if it wasn't because of the winds. But whether he heard me or not, I must speak. I must tell him something to sooth him. I was his elder friend and brother, at least for a while.

"Can you turn off the lights?"

"No, sir. This will be fatal. I won't see the road."

"Then tell the boys at the back to be silent. This is the same spot where we got those rebels this morning, don't you remember?"

"Yes, sir. I do remember very well. This is not the first time today for me to meet these women on this road. They are always here, but it seems they only ambushed passenger vehicles."

"No, you don't understand, captain. They have attacked several army vehicles, killing and wounding several of our people. For this reason, we don't have to underestimate the enemy, don't you understand?"

"Yes, sir. I perfectly understand. I think the best thing is for us to watch out because even if we don't speak, the pickup is loud enough for them to hear. We can't silence the vehicle, can we?"

"Our commander is a coward!"

"Shush! He'll hear you speak!"

"Don't forget the winds!"

I could hear these soldiers enduring the strong winds with us speak under their voices as much as they can. I can imagine how bad the commander might be if his own soldiers speak like this for the fear of him. It also seemed he never been in the frontlines. He might have been one of the recruits who never been at any real military training camps, but is now having high ranks. He seemed to be a true civilian, which is why he still thought along the tribal lines. But my thoughts might have been wrong. Even the well educated in Africa still thinks like those living deep in the villages. But is this only true in Africa? How about those in the Europe and the America, don't they have their own tribes? At least, I was speaking out of experience. Since I never been in either Europe, or America, I had no idea how things were like in those parts of the world.

"What do you do to get out of these situations?" Yien asked as if he was still pondering over my words of encouragement. Now, I knew he was listening.

"I don't do anything much. Sometimes, I just allow the nature to take its course, and it does. Sometimes, I could speak up in their language, and a miracle happens. But I can't credit myself on all these techniques, simply because my life isn't in my own hands. Remember, Jesus told the then governor of his land that he could do nothing unless it was given him from above. This means that nothing dies at the wrong time, or in a wrong way. Have you ever tried to crush an ant which has just bitten you but couldn't? Do you remember how many times you kept missing it until in went away? Think about it. You and I are better than ants. We are better than sparrows. We are much better than birds and animals. This means we can't die unless our time has come. When our time comes, who can help us?"

Then it was time to see lights from a distance. I was Juba, from the eastern bank of the Nile River. We have just arrived. But we were dying from the pain. Our hands still stuck on our backs. The lights were coming closer and closer as we cruised on speed, but then fear seemed to have been thrown out of the pickup windows by the winds. We passed all the known spots where the rebels or bandits hid and attacked passing vehicles. I wondered why they were not captured and disarmed. Maybe they were strong enough to cause havoc in the area.

"Tie their eyes with pieces of cloth!" he shouted as the pickup comes into a sudden stop. Are they going to shoot us dead? This was the question both of us were asking as the men took some black clothes and tied our eyes without any warning.

CHAPTER 17

May 16th 1998, Kiech Kuon

"Why was the Sudanese government dropping bombs on the civil population of South Sudan in 1990s to 2001? I remember one incident when they dropped several bombs on the people and cattle alike. But, I didn't understand the relationship between those poor civilians and the rebels, can you tell me?"

"Boy, that's a weird question! You mean you don't yet know the connection between the two? But to answer your questions, the connection was that simple to know. Even the little children can guess what it is. The north hated the south ever since."

"But is this true?" I interrupt.

"Yes, and this was because their government was not ours. They didn't care to kill women and children. They wanted to do ethnic cleansing in the south," he went on and on to explain the reasons behind those merciless aerial bombardments by the government of Khartoum in those days.

"But by then, we were part of the whole country. We were Sudanese!" I explained.

"That didn't mean we were all Arabs or Muslims, did it? Being in the same territory or country doesn't always mean that you are the same people. We are not the same with them, even the British Condominium rulers knew the fact that we would have been better if we were given our own independence apart from that of the north. We are very different, both in race, as well as in culture and religion."

"I thought I still remember you saying that the attacks in the south were carried out, not because we were not Arabs, but that because of the rebellion in the south. Now, you are telling me that this was so because of the racial and religious reasons. Which one is true and which one is not?"

"Look, you have to see the context first. It's true that we had war, which was so complex to explain, because its causes were and are still many. Natural resources are always on the top of the list when it comes to the causes of any conflict in the world. But don't forget the issue of race, religion, and political power. Yes, there were rebels in the south in the 1990s, but the government of the day was also mainly composed of the Arabs. These people knew that one day one time, the south will become an independent state, and this isn't good news for them. Our people were, are, and will always be Africans, no matter what. We are neither Muslims nor Christians."

"But I am a Christian, grandpa! Why do you say this? Maybe you are not a Christian, but I am. My children are also going to be Christians after me and this will happen automatically without any external forces to intervene. I don't understand it when you say we are neither Muslims nor Christians. What do you mean?

"When I say we are neither Muslims nor Christians I mean to say the truth. Tell me, do you know that many of your pastors and elders, or whatever you call them, still go into their brothers or relatives houses to produce children for the deceased? Is this not a culture from the ancient world? Have you ever read about it in your Bible? This means if we do this, we are like the Jews in many ways. We are not Christians as the West defines Christianity today. This is what I mean. We are not Muslims because we don't always practice Islam in the same way Arabs do."

"Do you mean to say that Christianity is not the same in every continent?"

"Yes, my grandson. It is never the same. People actually believe in their own things and then they confuse them with foreign ideologies. In Africa, we are Africans. In the US, they are who they are. Their Christianity is different from ours simply because of the different cultures between us and them. If you also go to Asian countries, Christianity or Islam in those parts of the world differs a lot from what we have here or what they have there in the West. For this reason, the Arabs hated us because they knew who we really were from the inside-out. They still hate us and they will still hate us, no matter if we are Muslims or not. Islam is synonymous to the Arab culture. In the same way, Christianity, the very religion you now call yours, is synonymous to the Western cultures, simply because the West is almost hundred per cent influenced by the Jewish and Christian world views. However, they are still mixed people. America is known to be the land of the immigrants, and this means something. It means there is no single culture or religion in that part of the world. Their cultures and religions are mixed."

"So, whenever they dropped bombs on us, grandpa, does it mean they were killing animals because they knew we were not humans like them since we were neither Muslims nor Christians?"

"You have said it all, my dear grandson. They did it because they knew we are a different people. We are Africans and they are Arabs."

"But the Sudanese Arabs have been here since time immemorial. How do we even categorize them as Arabs today? If someone is born and raised in Africa, is he or she not an African?"

"No, he or she cannot and will never be an African simply because he or she was born in Africa. If her or his parents are Americans, he or she is an American regardless of where he or she was born and raised from. In the same way, the Arabs in the Sudan are and will always be Arabs. They came from Saudi, just as we came from Israel many years ago. We are Israelites. We are a tribe of Israel. You can confirm this through our oral history."

"How about the Ethiopians, are they Arabs as well?"

"Yes, they are. If you read their history books, which were never written, you will know where they came from. But unless you read that in the ether, a part of our universe, which is responsible for keeping everything from history. This is the true historian who never lies. You can lie. The ether won't lie. I can lie. Any human being can create their own assumptions over any given subject, but the ether won't. All the red people, including the Indians, are of Arab origin."

"I never heard, thought, or even imagine such a thing! I am thrilled as well as surprised by your very own conclusions, grandpa. Your teachings are hard to understand just like Paul's teachings are in the Bible. But, you are an elder, one of the elders of this country. How can I argue with you? But I still don't understand this mind-set."

"You will understand maybe when you are of age. For now, let me preach to you. You can't get the message, but it is that simple to understand when you grow older, or when you read and study more. Knowledge is not only found in a classroom.

Classrooms have their own forms of education and knowledge. But this is just a small fraction of what you learn from the world we live in, my son. Do you know that education, real education, is more than learning how to read and write in any known human language?"

"Yes, I know that education simply means learning how to do something and actually do it. But how do we relate education with the government of the Sudan dropping those killing machines called bombs on the civilian population of South Sudan in those days?"

"We came to the topic of education because I was trying to tell you that the reason the government did this horrible thing was to kill or scare away the people of this land. If we were scared, we would have abandoned our leaders in the bushes, thinking we can't fight against such a civilized people with what we had at hand. This would have stopped the rebellion altogether and there would have been no country called South Sudan today. Then I wanted you to know that God created us black, just as he created them brown, or red as we call them. This means all the brown or red people are Arabs, and the white people are the Linglith (English) people, while we the black are purely Africans of many different ethnicities. This is where the idea of education came in because I wanted you to know that for one to know these truths, he or she doesn't need to go to school, especially those modern schools where modernism rules the learning process."

"Now, I remember exactly how they used to drop those bombs on us, but God or luck took us through it all and we are here now. Is there anything you think we can do to create love and harmony among races?"

"I have no idea what could be done to create love, peace, or harmony among human races. Maybe nature was made to be that way. Maybe this is our ecosystem, at best. Maybe humans are meant to keep their balance in check, naturally in how they hate, fight and kill each other. Maybe this is the best way to keep our numbers low before we fill the planet earth and then we end up feeding on each other directly just as our brothers and sisters do in the wild."

"Who are those brothers and sisters in the wild?"

"Animals. Insects. Birds. Reptiles. All these and many others are part of this world, just as you and I are. We eat or feed on each other economically and in many other ways possible. But the rest of animals do it directly for their own reasons. In this way, the Arab-dominated government of the then Sudan cared less about us. But at the same time, they did bomb us because they were told rebels mixed up with the normal civilians, and to separate the two, the government must bomb those reported areas. But because they were also scared, they used to bomb us from very high up so they hardly see what they were aiming at. In most cases however, they even dropped bombs on cattle and they did it intentionally."

"Since we now have our very own country, is there any possibility that we will have good relationships with the Sudan?"

"The fact is that people everywhere still call us Sudanese, whether we like it or not. The name Sudan is not yet going anywhere, and I doubt if it will go anywhere sooner or later. For this reason, the two Sudans must have better relationships regardless of their hatred and racial differences. By the way, they are and they will always be bordering each other."

"Is this what it means when people say that the government politics are dirty games?"

"Yes, I would agree with you on principle. But we don't have to treat them in the same way they treated us. I also know that not all the Arabs hated us. Arabs are humans and there are no two different humans that agree on the same thoughts and beliefs. You can say this about any human race on the face of the earth. Just as there are good and evil people in every tribe, there are good and evil people in every human race."

CHAPTER 18

October 16th 2019, Juba

"We are dead. We are finished!" Yien spoke up.

"Calm down, young rebel! Calm down, my son. You have to face the law first before you ever meet your fate. We have a law. This is not the jungle you are familiar with. This is a country with laws and customs," he tried to prove he was doing his job.

"Untie their hands, not their eyes!" he said.

"Take them in and then come back. Our job is now done. We had to go to the best hotel and reward ourselves after our long day's work," he was saying this while looking at his relatively young men, the torturers. They seemed to love their job, but did they? Were they not forced to do this by this very situation that they were in? Were they different from anyone who is forced in to doing the very thing he or she hates the most?

I could hear the commander, or rather, the officer hitting the ground hardest with is foot as he handed us over to the higher authority before turning his back to his boss as swift as a soldier must do and then he left the premises as soon as he could.

"Take this to the room you know and take the other younger one to the other side of the prison. They must face the law soon," an unfamiliar voice roared. It was now crystal clear that we were under the authority of other men for the first ones have gone back to do their business. I can't tell which part of Juba we were in. But was this even important? Do we deserved to be in that situation in the first place?

The 26 days in prison were like 26 years in hell. I have forgotten about many details of my story. But when that day of release came, I recalled even the seemed forgotten things of my past. It was indeed a day like none other.

But in that blue house, a name that resembles that of the Blue Band, even though the content of that product is yellow, we saw what hell looked like, here on the planet earth. It's even horrible to recall those events without shedding hot tears. We have seen the redness of it all because we were branded as such.

I, Mut, have seen people die even those who lived, chat, ate and shared life with us for days. Their time came and they were taken away from us never to be seen again. They had committed crimes punishable by death. They had to be either hanged or shot at depending on who they were and what they did.

In the very night when Yien and I arrived at the prison, it took me time to see him again because we were not placed in the same place. The prison was meant for true criminals of which I don't qualify to be one. I was made into a criminal just like Jesus of

Nazareth was, but I was yet to be crucified. I thought Yien was no more. I was then relieved of that pain when I once saw him again. He was as innocent as a dove. His service even in that hell on earth was unique and special. The young man was different from the rest in many different ways.

"You get inside, sir," this kind-hearted young man invited me into a cell. He sounded so kind though I still had to learn more about him as days go by. It doesn't take that long to distinguish personalities from each other, does it? His tone of voice tells it all to his prisoners.

"Who are you, brother and where is this place?"

"I am not here to tell you anything about myself or about the place you are in right now. My very role is to take care of you until it's time for you to be taken to court. I don't know what crimes you have committed and I don't have the rights to ask you either," he went on.

I think he was doing his job, but was it his heart's desire to be there? Was this his career? Was money or other things not the factor behind, forcing him to do the dirty job? I can't bother him with many questions. Maybe I was somehow insane by then.

I had to enter the cell. I can tell many people have been there for too long. This was hell on earth. I don't think I deserved to be there since there was no reason. What have I done to be placed in that place? Anyway, there was nothing I could do right there. All I can do was to sit and then stand up whenever I was tired. The cell was too small like a well. If you have been digging wells in your life, then you know how narrow it was for a tall Cushite like myself. I had to be there for as long as nature could tell.

"Mut! Come out! It's time to take something. I know you must be hungry by now. Please come and eat with your other friends," a voice called from the outside of the cell. But I can't open the door myself. He had to do it. He knew.

Coming out of the cell, he had to lead me to the other room at least with fresh air to breath in. There were men from all parts of the country, including some foreigners. Men of different ages and walks of life. Some were modern-ly educated, and others were traditionally educated. Education comes in different shapes and colours so to speak. Being able to read and write in any human language is not the only thing called education. If you know how to create fire out of wood, then you are educated in doing just that.

"Hi, welcome on-board! What's your name?" A young man in red shorts and a blue shirt asked, looking at me in the eyes. I was alert.

"My name is Mut Peter from Unity State. I am a South Sudanese by birth. What's your name?"

"My name is Machiek, and I hail from Yirol. I am also a South Sudanese by birth." Now I was thinking about something. Is he from Malual Abongbar clan? He might have been from that Dinka section known of turning into carnivores at will. He might start to feast on other prisoners if he wants to. Or maybe these are olden day tell-tales? I hoped so.

"I have heard many stories about your people."

"Yeah, but not all stories are true. A human mind can imagine anything. This is how fiction stories were born. Don't believe everything, brother."

Right there we were feasting on some kind of Asida, not like the one we had in the Upper Nile. It was that kind called Ugali in East Africa. We are East Africans, too. At least, we are a part of this region, politically as well as businesswise. But still our Asida doesn't look and taste like that one. At least we had something to eat. It has been two days or more before I tasted any food.

"My name is Lokiri, and I am from Kajo-keji." I heard it the other way, 'Hajo-heji', and I understood what the words meant. They meant a lost calf. Could this be the same name, Marakal now turned into Malakal or Malbakal? Anyway, each person had his or her own stories to tell about the meaning of these words and places, and that was another conflict of its own. "Call me Alex, and I am from Kenya. I am a

Kenyan citizen by birth. But now we are all here. Nations and tribes don't matter right now, do they? We are all one in this prison. At least we are prisoners and that is what matters the most at the moment. We are but a tribe of criminals whether we like it or not."

I was thinking about something. Jesus, the Saviour was among the criminals of His day though He was not a criminal in the real sense. Maybe some of us there were true criminals, but not all of us were. Yet, he was right. They thought we were all criminals and that was why they placed us in the prison and then they mistreated us all.

"Where is my friend, Yien?"

"Oh, he's in a different place. You mean the young man who came with you last night? I saw him being dragged into another cell, which is not very far from here. But he is in another group. Don't worry about him. By the way, I am Kun, and I come from Nasir. I am a South Sudanese by birth."

Then the bell was ringing. This meant we had to hurry up. It was almost time to get back into our individual cells. It was where we sweat copiously and craved just enough oxygen to keep us breathing.

Hell!

One of the men there was in the prison because he impregnated a woman and her elder daughter. This was a serious crime in this part of the world. A woman was someone else's wife. A woman's daughter was someone else's daughter, too. These were two different crimes altogether. But the same husband to the woman was the daughter's dad. His wife committed adultery and his daughter was defiled according to his worldview. This man must be punished by law. By that time, law meant what a traditional court ruled even in the then capital city. There were no national laws per se. Each state had her own laws. The husband to that woman was so kind otherwise, he would have killed the man who was now in prison because he caught them on action.

Another young man was there because he had killed his own mother. He seemed to have been in his right mind. But what does it mean to be in the right mind? Is there anything like being right in this world? If they could take me in to that place without any investigations, is there anything called right?

"The time is up!" she shouted the last warning and we had to be taken back or rather, we had walk back to our cells. These were narrow rooms with no ventilations whatsoever. Good enough, I had my Bible and a hymnbook. I could read about three to four books in the Bible per day and sang about four different songs. But my books were getting wet from my own sweat. Whenever I was back to my cell, I had to think about life. Meditation was encouraged in the prison cells. I had to think of the here and the now, not forgetting the past. But I didn't have to worry about the past mistakes or anticipate much about the unknown future. I didn't know what will happen to me next. Will they sentence me to death without a trail? I have heard such stories of people being taken out of their cells never to be seen again. Execution there was not in any possible way, including being shot and thrown into a hole. Sometimes, I was told they break your neck and do away with your dead body. No trails. No hearing.

But I wanted to always take time to think about this beautiful country. When are we going to collect taxes and use it for development? When are we going to use the immigration money for development? Who eats the money paid at all our borders? We have borders with the Sudan, Ethiopia, Kenya, Uganda, Congo, and Central Africa Republic. All people from these countries entered our country with a visa.

Why are the landing fees so high at our airports compared to those in other countries? Where is our oil money? Is it true as I was made aware that some individuals divide the oil cash among themselves at the airport before it reaches to the central bank?

CHAPTER 19

November 26th 2006, Malakal

"I know the fact that there were so many militias in South Sudan during the main civil war. Now, what caused the battle of Malakal, which took place towards the end of November 2006?" I asked. "Boy, there were many causes to that battle. They accused Gen. Gabriel Tang Ginye to be the cause, but that wasn't true. There was a reason for him to attack the then the SPLA positions in the southern parts of the town such as Gisa Jinubi," he explained.

"Yes, but the Sudanese Armed Forces (SAF) responded with heavy artilleries afterwards, which means this was a coordinated kind of a battle. What was the connection between the SAF and Tang?" I asked, looking at the old man in the eyes.

"Sometimes you ask questions as if you are not a trained professional journalist. It seems you are a government agent to ask me questions so that you reveal these secrets to the government of South Sudan. But I don't care what the purpose may be. I will always give you my answers as best as my old memory can recall," he went on.

"No, I want to ask professional questions. Sure, I am not a journalist, and I don't plan to become one. I just need facts. I want to know what happened and why it happened. They say history keeps repeating itself, and I think we can avoid this fate in the future if we know our history very well. So what happened?" I explained myself to an old man already in a rage.

"Listen now!" he commanded before he resumed. "The SPLA from the southern side of the town attacked Tang and his forces first, chasing them to the Sudan government's side. Then the Sudanese government soldiers had to respond in self-defence. That was what happened. It was not Tang who started the fight against anyone, but this was how the media reported it," he resumed.

"What I don't understand very well, grandpa is that each and every person tells their own version of the same events. Who do I believe at the end?"

"Well, you will have to decide who to believe in at the end of the day, or is it the end of life?"

"That's what confuses me the most. How do I make a decision when everyone seems to have a different narration of the same events? In fact, even the names of places such as Malakal have different meanings to different people with their own unique interests. I remember reading a book in the 1990s which seems to say, "Tɛɛ̈t, Malakal, Shilluk, Naath, Nuär, Nasir," and so on and so forth. What do you know about this? Is such a book historically factual or was it fictional? Does it mean that those tribes mentioned owned those places? Is there a place called Nasir in South Sudan?"

"Son, I don't know about those names and about those books or that book you have read in the 1990s. But I can tell you that that's another problem in itself. Let's talk about the first questions instead. You wanted to know where were there so many militias in South Sudan in the 1990s, didn't you?"

"I was particularly asking about the battle in that town. You know, I was there in person. But as always, I have been wondering about the real cause since then. There are many different stories about the battle. Even some of the soldiers who fought there seem to have no idea at all about what happened."

"Sure, now you are back to the topic. I can tell you that the cause or rather, causes were many. Just as it was, it is still true today that our people can fight for their own reasons. Rumours spread much faster than truth in the country. I am sorry to say this but this is the truth. Our people love to spread false allegations and accusations much faster than telling the truth."

"Are you saying you don't know what or who was behind this battle?"

"I don't know the answers because I don't want to point fingers at others. Look, they used to say that the more you point one finger to others, you will always end up pointing more fingers at yourself," he said this while laughing out loud. He then looked back at me before checking on his white rope, the *Milaya* clothing he wore when the heat goes high in the Upper Nile region. This was one of the hottest places in this country apart from Juba.

"I also don't know why you are asking me. Maybe you want these people to be taken to the international criminal court one day. Maybe that's why you are asking. You know, in these days, children can even sell out their parents for money. I don't want to be in prison for saying such things. I want to die in peace, not in pieces," he said as he smiled widely before laughing out loud again. The man keeps himself happy by sharing his stories with others whenever possible. He was a historian by nature. He seemed to enjoy his career though he didn't get paid in any currencies.

"As usual, I want to know who was being the battle and why. This is how history is made. I want young people to know what happened and why it happened."

"I agree with you, my grandson. I know you want to know these details for your own reasons. But do you think every other human being thinks like you do? Most humans don't understand issues in the same way as you and I do. Anything can be misunderstood for an insult, even if you never imagined such a thing when you talked about these events. In our day and age, one has to be extra careful, my son. You may end up in our prisons where there is no trial or hearings about your case. Who cares?"

"You are right, grandpa. But this kind of behaviour doesn't stop brutality and crimes, does it? Can't we still know the right from wrong? Look, people have their own stories to tell about such major events in our country. Most of these stories are false because they were based on hearsay, not on actual accounts. This is sad for people like me."

"Do you know that humans love such made up stories more than the reality? This is why people read fiction works more than they do history. And even what we call history is not accurate enough to the actual details. We humans do forget things faster. This means whenever we tell stories, we miss out a lot of detail. Worse still, we tend to forget the most important facts. This is fact, not fiction."

"At least you might know what happened exactly, especially about this battle. I want to know the truth. I want to share this truth with others."

"And I had told you the truth. They made it up. What you know is not the truth. This is why most, if not all people in this country will always believe in lies. Do you know there are so many myths already about our current leaders such as Dr. Riek Machar?

Have you not heard a story about how he steals a Boing 737 from Khartoum International Airport? But was he even a pilot? Do you know if he did his doctorate in what? Answer me, young man!"

"Yes, I used to hear those stories in 1990s, and I thought they were real until recently. I think he got his doctorate in agriculture, right?"

"You are wrong, my son. You don't know. He got his PhD in Strategic Planning in Industry from a UK university, Bradford. He never studied aviation in his life. Maybe in the future. Therefore, he can't steal a plane without any piloting knowledge. It's also amazing because in that story, we are not told where he was taking the plane and why. But this means out of imagination, we humans create stories. Even most, if not all of our decisions are based on emotional choices, not on rational thinking."

"Could this be the same way we get those biblical stories such as the virgin birth?"

"If We had to tell the truth, yes. Most, if not all stories in the Bible are fiction. Even the creation story is not literal. It's pure fiction, but who wants to admit that, anyway? Who wants to be crucified? Truth crucifies. The foolish majority will burn you alive."

"Does it mean because the truth crucifies, we then can't tell the truth about who was behind the battles in different places in this country?" I asked. I still wanted to know his answers. Before he jumped in to answer me he first looked away then back on me. I don't know what that gesture meant. Maybe he wanted me to pay attention?

"Yes, you're right. Telling the truth needs some kind of wisdom otherwise. Especially in those country, you have to carry your cross after telling the truth. We don't have freedom of speech because most people are likely to misunderstand you and you will end up in the Blue House."

"What's that Blue House?"

"It's a house in Juba where criminals are kept and punished by the National Security. This is not a security as such but a group of wise people who are in unity to eat people's money in their own ways."

"How about that story of Gatluak Manguel, or was it Panguel?" I asked. "Whatever name you want for his father, Pa-nguel, or Pa-ngeng, it's still another myth, my grandson. There are no historical records about this carnivorous human-like creature called Gatluak. The story is fictional, just like that of Panyim of Nyar-kueth."

"Really? I think many people still believe in those stories in some parts of South Sudan today and saying these are fiction is like a blow in their faces! How about those who say they themselves witnessed the people from Malual Abongbar clan to have been eating people, what can we say about them? Can we verify their stories in real life? Can people also make up such painful stories? I have heard stories such as that of Nyaliu, a Dinka Ngok lady who was believed to have been married to one of those Bahr el Ghazal people, who then wanted to eat her and then she managed to escape. I heard that these wild humans used to come and cry with her name, 'Nyaliu oou, Nyaliu oou,' the whole night for years, looking for her. What can you say about such stories?"

"No matter how many people believe in those tales, I don't because they are just tales. None of those people will tell you they have heard these voices themselves. They will tell you they heard about it somewhere and that proves it wrong."

"I am thrilled to hear more!"

"That's good. I will then tell you more. The fact is that it is very complex to know who is saying what in this world. That's why even the real causes of our civil wars are unknown to be exact. But it is clear that our human nature is the real cause of all evil in the world. But how this evil nature came about is every man's guess. Many stories have been created to tell us what it is and where it came from. But all these stories are absolutely fictional at best."

CHAPTER 20

November 21st 2015, Kampala

"How much is it from here to the airstrip?"

"Fifty South Sudanese Pounds, sir," says the bodaboda rider. The distance to Yei airstrip was one hour walk but about 20 minutes by the motorcycle, also known as a bodaboda, an East Africa word.

The journey was for an international conference for the church leaders and partners from around the world. Then from Addis, I had to take a flight to Lagos. On my way to Lagos, Nigeria, I had to take a flight from Entebbe, Uganda, to Addis Ababa, Ethiopia. Before reaching to Entebbe, I had to use a motorcycle to a small airport in Yei, South Sudan. Then from Yei, I had to fly to Juba, the then capital city.

"When is the plane coming?"

"I think about ten minutes from now," said a passenger-to-be. He seemed to be going to Juba for something very important based on how he dressed. But some people love their dress codes even if they are not in any business. We all have our dressing codes based on who we are, naturally. He might be going there for his own reasons. The road to Juba was no longer secure by this time. People were selected on tribal bases and were mercilessly killed by unknown gunmen in the country. Peace was only a dream so to speak. Anyone who can afford the air transport must opt for it.

"How far is it from here to Juba by air?"

"It's about 20 minutes, sir," he says. About one hour of waiting, we had to board the caravan passenger plane. There were two Ugandan pilots, all were males. Taking off as usual, I could see the mobile house leaving the earth, grass, anthills, rocks, trees, hills, mountains and clouds. I could see the beauty of the landscape. And about 20 minutes on air, we arrived to Juba International Airport, the JIA. This was the biggest and the best international airport in the whole country apart from that in Paloch in the Upper Nile State.

"Welcome to Juba, sir. May I have your luggage?" a young man asked. He wore a T-shirt with words printed on the back, 'I love South Sudan,' and I wished he still does. After giving him my bags, we entered the car and left for a pastor's home in town.

"Welcome brother Mut!"

"Thank you, sir. How are you doing?"

"We are doing well. We are blessed. We are a chosen generation, a royal priesthood. Welcome to Juba," says the pastor.

"We will spend the night here. But early in the morning, We had to leave for Kampala, Uganda. You and other team members will have to travel by a bus. I will follow you on the same day by air. Have you ever been to Uganda before?" asks the pastor.

"Yes, I have been at the Ugandan border. I was in Moyo in 2011 when one of our pastors passed on in Kampala and we had to receive his body from there."

"Oh, sorry. That was a bad experience."

"Yes, it was. But anyway, I was there. I never been deep into Uganda before. I don't even know how far is Kampala from Juba."

I had to celebrate someone's birthday that day. One of her gifts was to attend the international conference in Lagos, Nigeria. It was a great way to show love and compassion for each other as a family.

"How will we go from here to the bus park?"

"Someone will take you to the bus park."

In the next morning, we had to go to the bus park, which was located on the other side of the Nile River at a place called Shirkat. The bus had to pass through Nimule, a town in the border between South Sudan and Uganda. But was this the real border? Before Sudan split into two countries, was this the border? What is leading to this annexation of our country?

"How long is it from here to Nimule?"

"It takes three full hours from here to there," said the bus driver. This seemed to be the biggest and the fastest buses in the country. The road too was one of the only tarmac roads connecting the county to its neighbouring countries. The second road was that of Renk (Arang) in the northern Upper Nile region connecting the country to Sudan. At that time, there was no tarmac road to Ethiopia, Kenya, DRC, and to the C.A.R.

On the way, I could see that there were different trees, grass, landscapes and people. In Nimule, I had to give them my passport so they could stamp it with an exit stamp. They had to do the same on the Ugandan side, but differently.

"Hi, Peter," he greeted me.

"Hi, sir," I responded.

"Are you a teacher?"

"Yes, sir."

"How long are you going to be in Uganda?"

"I will be here for three months, sir."

"Okay, welcome to Uganda!"

"My pleasure!"

Then he gave back my passport with an entry visa attached. I had to pay $100 for it, a lot of money, right? That was how much I had to pay. Then on the way, I could hear birds sing whenever the bus comes to a stop somewhere in the forest. I could distinguish between male birds singing to other females, males singing to other males, and males singing alone. It seemed those who sang to themselves were teaching themselves how to sing or were simply rehearsing. They sang to impress females. They sang to other males to tell them they were present and that they were heroes in the forest. Females loved those who knew their art well and would love to befriend them more than those they liked less or didn't like at all.

"Are you a Sudanese?" she said with a wider smile on her face. I first didn't know what she meant, but I had to answer her, anyway.

"Yes, and no. I was a Sudanese, but now I am not. Rather, I am a South Sudanese?"

"But what is the difference between the two?"

"The difference is that there is nothing like North Sudan, therefore, South Sudan is not a part of that country called Sudan. Sudan is a different country since 9th July, 2011. This is 2015, and that's four years into our independency, and you still don't know we are a country of our own? This is amazing. I thought all our neighbouring countries knew this," I was trying to explain the issue.

"I think he's right. We are Sudanese. It doesn't matter if we come from the South or from the North. There's no need to argue about this because it won't make sense at all, no matter how we try our luck," said a young South Sudanese man on board, who was listing to our conversation on the same bus. "No, I don't think he's right. Maybe the language is the issue here. As he said, there's a huge difference between South Sudan and South Korea. This means in the former, there's no North, but in the latter, there is a North, meaning there are two parts of the same country. For us, we only have South Sudan but there is nothing called North Sudan. Also, if you have to travel to Sudan right now as a South Sudanese, you must go with your passport. This means we are not part of Sudan," a South Sudanese young woman responded to our conversation.

"Yes, you are right, my sister. That's the point."

"But why are you still fighting against each other? Were the Arabs the problem in your country?" he asked, looking at me now in the eyes. I can see some surprise, mixed with anger and some rage in his eyes. I just don't know if I knew the answers to his good questions. Maybe I was asking the same questions?

"I don't know the right answers to these questions, if there are right answers at all. But I think the situation is complex. We are fighting for the presidential seat, which means a lot. It means power. It means fame and wealth to become a president in Africa. Or is this the same thing in the world?"

"You people are full of hate. This is the reason why you stamped the movement on the back when we were about to win the war. If we captured Sudan by force in the 1990s, we would have been well known by now, everywhere. But you Nuer are hopeless people. You know how to fight very well whenever you want to. You also know how to negotiate well. But you have one problem. You don't study the situation before you take action, and this is why we Dinka will always be your rulers. Whenever you want to make a political change, you always make it tribal. Instead of attacking the government, you attack the Dinka people. You even have a song that goes, "*Kamda kɛ jaŋ /thile malesh*," and I think this is a mind-set like that of the Nazi Germany. You will never win in this country," the young South Sudanese man went on, looking at me in the eyes.

"Look at how they speak up against each other, pointing fingers against each other. Will there be peace in your country?" asked a Ugandan woman on board, looking at both of us, me and the other young South Sudanese man who have just spoke his mind.

"Look at you, our men. When are you going to forgive and forget the past? The Dinka can't forget. The Nuer always wants to revenge. This is going on forever. Are you like the Israelites and the Palestine in South Sudan?" asked the South Sudanese young woman who commented a short while ago on the difference between Sudan and South Sudan.

"I think you are the problem, not the Arabs. Even in the Sudanese civil wars you were fighting your own war within the bigger war between the north and the south, am I right?" asked the first Ugandan man who spoke up in the first conversation. He seemed to be right though. If indeed the problem was the Arabs, how come we were still fighting against each other after the Arabs left us? Why were we fighting over the leadership seat of the country, which we can boldly call our own? These questions kept raising other questions as well, not answers. It also seemed that all our neighbours looked down on us.

"I honestly don't know the answers, sir."

"You have to know the answers to these questions otherwise, there's no need to think you are a country of your own. Look, all food in your country is provided by this piece of land called Uganda. You can't compare this small country with even one of your regions in terms of size and even soil fertility, but when are you going to grow your own food? Do you think like humans?" the Ugandan man spoke.

"Give the country leadership to a woman and see the changes you need. Men seem to be defensive instead of thinking about a country they fought and died for. Your women are peaceful than your men. I can see this truth wherever I go. I do business in South Sudan and I know what I mean," she went on. That Ugandan woman was right, wasn't she?

CHAPTER 21

April 4th 2012, Panthou, South Sudan

"Why do the Sudanese people rename our places with names we the southerners don't understand? They call this place, Heglig, which has no meaning at all to the real owners. Can you explain why this was so?" I ask him, looking at him in the eyes. The old man looked at me and shook his grey head before he smiled and then tried to say one or two things.

"They do so for several reasons. One reason being that the Arabs can't either pronounce, nor spell a name such as Pan-thou correctly. They just can't. Thus, they renamed it in their language. This was the same thing with Nasir, Khartoum, Jebelen, etc. And, also, the Arabs and the Linglith (English) people can't remember our African names after some time. The natural logic was to rename them to things they could write, say, or remember," he explained.

I then went astray for a while from the topic and I was then thinking of how South Sudanese were given either Muslim or Christian names. Would this be for the same reason? Are there things like Muslim or Christian names in the first place? Are these not just Arab or Western names at best? "Ha, so there we go! I exclaimed after coming back from my wandering tour into the inner world of myself and my past events. The old man too seemed to have been wandering for a while. "They named me, Peter. But my real name is Mut, and you know what that means, right? It sounds like a Chinese name. The Chinese have names like ours, such as Deng, Tang, Bol, and many others," I explain.

"Yes, and they did that for the same reasons I have just told you. The Arabs can't spell, say, or remember your name, even though it's a very short and simple name to both you and me. This is the same reason why they renamed our places. And, the other reason of course is that they also claimed they owned the places, especially after the oil discovery in those places in the south in the 1970s. The US research for the oil in our land began in 1959 from the Red Sea littoral," he went on.

I was now thinking. The Arabs and the Westerners wanted to rename our places simply because they couldn't manage to say, remember, or spell our names. This is something amazing. I can see that my American or European friends can't say a female name like Nyakong correctly. But we can't pronounce their names correctly, too, can we?

I still wondered if this could also be a reason enough to rename places. Well, the old man was putting it right. They also did this to create history. This is how African history was altered and today,

Google will try to complete the sentence for you when you type something like Africa has… into its search engine. Indeed, Africa has its own history in its own ways.

"Are the Arabs Sudanese?"

"Yes, and no, depending on who you are asking."

"And I am asking you!"

"I know. They are our cousins. Their forefathers came from Saudi Arabia, many years ago, and then they intermarried with us, Africans, especially, the Nubians. Have you never read the history of the Sudan? Well, they have altered a lot of that history by now. Yes, they are now Sudanese, but they were not. They came from their Arab world. We can trace them back to their origins, if needed," he explained.

"But then, how did they get in to the highest level of leadership in the Sudan?"

"Well, a lot of things happened leading to them climbing up into the leadership ladder. Do you know that there are several Arab tribes in the Sudan? These tribes fought against each other for centuries. This created a hierarchy in the system long before the English people came into the country. Those on the top of leadership were then of course given the leadership of the country when the Western system of civilization started. In those days, people used to lead themselves in a different way. There was nothing like democracy, or is it a demon-crazy? We had chiefdoms in the south, but they had kingdoms in the north. Some of our tribes in the south had kingdoms, too such as the Shilluk Kingdom, Funj Kingdom, etc."

"Why do you call it a demon crazy?"

"It is a demon crazy because there are so many kinds of democracy, and none of them proved to be effective for Africa. For example, the American democracy is not the same as the democracy in other Western countries both in form and in practice. Democracy is a politicized word, just like human rights and gender-based violence."

"What do you think about human rights?"

"I don't think each human society don't know what is right and wrong for themselves. Therefore, they don't need someone from the other end of the earth to come and tell them what their human rights are. But this is how humans are foolish enough in their nature. There is nothing like human rights because what is right is relative. It's right for a Western lady to walk in the public half naked. It's not right in Africa to do that. Even in those days, we tried to cover those parts of ours called private. But today, you don't even know which parts are private and which ones are public."

I had to think about this statement for a while. I didn't know how the world would react if I decide to wear a skirt and a blouse and then walk on our streets. I guess even dogs may start to bark at me. I can only imagine cameramen and women running after me to have the best shots. I can only imagine how the press will go wild about the act. I don't know what the religious institutions will say about this event.

"What about the gender-based violence?"

"This is another business plan by the West. Have you ever heard of African organizations working in the West? There are none. You might want to argue that this can't happen simply because Africa is poor and underdeveloped, but that's nonsense. The GBV is simply a Western project. This is how money is collected in the West for the West to study Africa better. They want to know what minerals you have and the best way to do this is to enter deeper into Africa, especially in to the African villages, so that they can do research at will."

"Then how about the churches?"

"The Church as well as other institutions have the same agenda. They exist to penetrate Africa for study and research. Do you know how many white men and women are living in our remote villages in South Sudan? Why are they in those villages where we have gold and other minerals? They are there in the name of evangelism and discipleship, but is that true? I don't think they are there for any ministry rather than that of their own. They are doing research. Most of them are American spies. Some are university students of geology and other vital subjects. Some have a plan and that plan is to find out where these valuable minerals are and they or their grandchildren will come to mine them later on. This is all I know, my son. You are free to believe me or not to."

"Do you think or believe that colonisation comes in different forms and colours? What can we do to stop both the West and the East from colonising our Africa again and again?"

"The answer depends on you, the Africans. You need to open your eyes. Why do you think Chinese keep coming to work in Africa? Do you Africans see what they see in Africa? Why are you people running to the West, thinking it's the only safe haven? It is because you don't see how rich your Africa is. It is because your leaders in Africa still think like slaves, and thus, they don't see how wealthy they are. They then keep looking for help from the outside world."

"How does this relate to the renaming of our places by both the Arabs and the English people?"

"I think there is a link between the two. The link is that they want to rename those places to change our history. They don't know Africa existed long before they came here. We had our own lives without them and their modernism ideas. But can we stay away from their views and lifestyles? This is a difficult question to answer because you people don't even know you have your own system of education. You do have your own cloth designs but now forgotten. Yes, they want to rename your places to make you think differently. It means that modern names are better than yours but are they?"

"What do you mean by their life?"

"You know. Life is more than being alive, physically. Life is a word that encompasses thoughts, words, and deeds. Life is culture. When I say their views and life I meant to say how the Westerners think and live their lives. Today, technology is everywhere, and it is influencing people's lives. But do you know that the Western culture is embedded on this technology?"

"But how does technology link to a culture?"

"That's exactly what I am trying to say. You can't even imagine how these two are related, yet you call yourself an educated person. Can't you see the link between the two? Yes, technology in itself is not cultural, but anyone can use it to spread his culture, and this is what the creators, the Westerners are doing. They embed things like individualism and capitalism in technology. But there is a huge need for social life, simply because we humans are social animals. Think about time management and how this separates the individual from the crowd. This idea is embedded into the modern education system and in technology. There are self-development courses everywhere online. These are good and evil at the same time. They are evil if they make you believe in your own abilities to the point of not seeing a need for others in your own world—selfishness."

"Do you mean self-discovery is selfish?"

"Yes, it is selfishness in most cases. It teaches you to know yourself beyond your weaknesses and needs. It makes you look down on other people and at the end of the day, you will begin to love yourself more than you love others. You will begin to think that only you can do it better."

I was speechless. I didn't know if I could tell the oldest man that I found it hard to both agree and disagree with his points. I had to remember the gap between us. He was my father's father. He was from a different generation altogether. Maybe he was right. Maybe he was wrong at some point. I didn't know why we allowed other people to rename our places at will. But they were our bosses. They used force to rename them. Even today, we don't remember how those names were pronounced or spelled, let alone the meaning behind them.

CHAPTER 22

July 16th 2011, Kakuma, Kenya

"Are you going to Nairobi?"

"Yes, and you?" she asked.

"I'm going there, too, but for the first time," I responded, looking away from her. She seemed to be alert and surprised at the same time.

"How far is Nairobi from Juba?"

"It takes about two hours by air, but this also depends on the plane speed and other factors," she explained. Her responses to my questions prove her character. She looked alert and confident on herself more than any other lady I ever met for the first time. She looked extroverted as well.

We had to wait there in the departure room of the terminal after a successful check-in with the Fly540 airliner. I seemed to have had more courage to look at her whenever she seemed to be focusing her attention on something or someone else. But I pretended to look away as soon as I sensed she was detecting this.

"Have you been in Nairobi before?"

"Yes, I have been there. Many times. I studied from there for years. I even know their language, Swahili. It's my second home, just as it is for many South Sudanese. I feel at home whenever I am there. I am even anticipating being there already. I can't help but imagine the place and everything in it such as trees, its coldness, and its people," she explained.

I can see most of the passengers were still away. I hoped they will join us sooner because the boarding time was approaching as we spoke. I hoped the pilots and the crew members will understand the fact that there seems to be no hurry in Africa, is there?

Both of us seemed to wander away at some point for some reasons. She looked young and active. Her hair was just natural, no additions. It was long and black. She seemed to take care of it daily. Is she from different races? Does it mean she was using some good hair shampoo? All these were my own guesses.

"Where did you go to school?" she asked.

"Here in South Sudan."

"Oh, but your English is very good!"

"Yeah, just as your hair is very good, and I guess you are a South Sudanese by birth, aren't you?" she smiled after hearing these words, and then looked at me in the eyes. I felt somehow nervous whenever she tried to do this to me much longer. Her dark pupils with white cornea make me feel some love and innocence in her part. She looked generous and lovely. She looked peaceful to be around though she seemed to talk a bit louder than I am. I had to resist this temptation to go closer or ask her of her phone number or email address. If we get on the plane, she might be sitting far away from me and I won't be able to get in touch with her forever. She was an angel, at least from her outside look and feel. She also looked too young to be married. Maybe she just completed her studies. But why was she going back to Kenya at the end of the year?

Before long, other passengers were arriving to the waiting room. There were also some calls through the big speakers on the ceiling over ahead. Then this man seemed to have his eyes on her too, and this puts me off. As an introverted being, I can't compete well with other men. In those olden days, people of my kind could hardly keep their females for long.

"Come, follow me!" Says a lady on the airliner's uniforms. We had to follow after her as she led us into the airport where the plane was waiting for us. It was a short walk of about a hundred metres from the terminal. My lady seemed to have noticed my feelings after someone intrusive than me came in between.

Before we entered the plane, we had to check if our bags were there. They were placed somewhere near the plane. Whenever you confirm all your bags were there, they were separated with other people's bags and they ask you to enter the plane. We were entering one person at a time. The ladder seemed to carry a certain weight, just like the plane itself. Soon, we would be airborne. I can imagine how it will be when on air for about two hours. I have been flying within and outside the country several times before. But this was my first time to fly to Nairobi.

"Welcome on board!" one of the ladies, a crew member, announced as we entered the airliner. The plane was big enough to carry about a hundred people or more. All seats were full to the brim. I had to carry my computer bag with me and never put it into the opening above my head. I had to keep it in front of me where I was seated. I was trying to see where she will be sitting. Good enough, her seat happened to be 24 B, when mine was 24 A. I was at the window and she sat on my right hand side.

Luck?

"Hey, we are together?" she asked, looking at me again in the eyes though I was trying to look away towards the window on my left hand side.

"Yeah, it seems there's something unique about this journey and us, what do you think?" I was trying to look at her now and she was smiling widely. I hoped I was not going to lean towards her and do something foolish. I can't look at her shining eyes for a minute or else, I don't know what will happen if I do so.

"Are you Nuer?" she asked, leaning towards me pretending to be looking at the window at the same time instead of answering my question about something about us and the journey. I could feel something like electric current running down my spine as I tried to ignore her and her question. Then she pulled back to her seat as she searched for the seatbelt, adjusting it to her size. She was that medium. She was neither huge nor was she too slim either.

"You're right. But I would rather like to be identified as a South Sudanese. I think our country is beautiful enough to be our identity, what do you think?" I was now looking at her in the eyes. At least this looked like a private place.

"Me, too. I am Nuer. But why do you want to be identified as a South Sudanese? You are a Nuer first before you become a South Sudanese, aren't you? Are you men so afraid of the Dinka nowadays that you don't even want to describe yourselves as Nuer even when you are still Nuer in your blood?" she asked, looking at me in the eyes. Trying to look at the window, I could see that this was Juba bridge. This means the plane took off without my knowledge. It took off northwards and then it turned west then southwards to cross the Nile River as it headed towards Kenya, and that was southeast.

"I won't get married to a Nuer man if this is the case. You men are coward," she resumed while I was enjoying the plane's climb over the clouds. I was able to see the beauty of the land. Vast areas looked like small compounds. They were very green and fertile even from 37 feet above the sea level. What a country? What a blessed land that flows with milk and honey? But are our people enjoying this land and her resources as they should? What can I do to help bring peace in the land? Do I have a role to bring peace?

"Can we talk now?" she asked.

"Yes, we can talk, sister. I am just enjoying the landscapes of our beautiful country. It's as beautiful as you are, isn't it?" I was now looking at her again in the eyes. She smiled and tried to look away. At lease that made her shy away for a while. Maybe I was making things clear to her now. But that natural and traditionally braided loom of hair was killing me. Can I touch it? What if that ends in a fight or in a terrible screaming? What if others behind us and those across the plane could see me do this? These thoughts were racing in my mind. I didn't know what to do.

"I know that I am a Nuer. But I am also a South Sudanese at the same time. What do you think is much better than the other? I better be brave for a good course. When we fought for our independence, there was a reason for that war. But what's the reason for our own war?" she seemed to be listening because she was looking away from me by then. She was looking at her fingernails that were so natural, no modern colours. "What do you do professionally?"

she was asking, looking at me again at this time. But I was still wondering why her voice changed as well as her way of looking at me from those first ones. I could tell the change in both her voice and her posture because I was deeply an empath. I seem to feel and care about other people's emotions as well as those of mine, so quickly.

"I am a teacher by profession."

"What do you teach?"

"I teach many things, such as languages, IT, and life coaching. I love it when I teach the youth about the importance of life and self-discovery. I love it when I work alone, using technology."

"Indeed, I agree. You are a teacher, and we need more people like you in this country. I was looking at you carefully when I first asked for your opinion. I wanted to know how you were going to react to my questions. I hate this hate speech that you find everywhere, including the online world. Our young people, including myself, will be blessed to have people like you to speak to them. But where will you do this? Do we have such venues in South Sudan? Will they not think you're holding a political rally, if you call and address the youth anywhere in our country?" she was now speaking while looking at her beautiful hands on the other seat in front of her. The crew members kept interrupting us from time to time.

This means we kept silent for some time before we resumed our sweet talk mixed with love and politics and patriotism. It seemed each human has some political views, just as each one of us has some theological views. This is because both politics and theology are social sciences. In fact, theology was once called the queen of all sciences in those olden days. After landing at the Jomo Kenyatta International Airport in Nairobi, Kenya, on October 21st 2016, I had to stay for some months with friends in Nairobi before taking a visit to the refugee camp in the northern part of the country. This means I had to renew my visa several times to make it stay valid while living in a foreign land. Here, I could see and hear how our neighbours ridicule South Sudanese.

But can I blame those who ridicule us? Are we not living in all countries both near and far? When we live in these countries, don't we show our true colours?

Our neighbours seem to know this weakness. They always say something to make us angry and use that anger as an offense so that we pay for our own sins. Then when in prisons, we had to call our friends and relatives who then send the money to the police so we that are to be released from the prisons.

CHAPTER 23

November 12th 2019, Juba

I don't know the answers to my questions, but I have to think and keep thinking as long as I breathe. Our government seems to be very busy doing all it could to make sure there is no physical infrastructure. If civilians could still buy firearms to use them for self-defence, then what's the work of the government? Who protects who? In the world, the government protects her citizens, not citizens protecting themselves and their properties. But in my country, it's the role of a civilian to sell his cows and goats in order to buy arms. Who is selling them these arms? Are they always using them for self-defence?

If you happen to share your thoughts on how we can together build the country, you may lose your head. Every day, they bring people in as they take others out for either execution or release.

This kind of life went on for about a month. However, I could see that there is true unity in our prisons then there is outside these cells. There is no Nuer or Dinka, neither Shilluk nor Bari in these prison cells. Each prisoner seems to think more about life and death rather than this useless tribalism.

"Mut, come out!" he commanded. I still didn't know his real name. But his kindness has given him a name that I won't forget for the rest of my life: peace. Something strange. He was with a policewoman in full uniforms. Are they going to execute me today?

"I am coming!" I responded as I prepared to leave the ever heating cell. It has been so hot even when it rained outside. This was Juba, anyway.

"You have been declared not guilty according to the law. This means you can now pack and go home. Do you know anybody in Juba?" asked a policewoman I was seeing for the first time though I have been there for the last twenty and so days.

"Madam. Since I was brought in, there's no trial or hearing. Now, you are telling me to just go home? Why am I here in the first place? What crime have I committed?"

"Mut. You are not supposed to ask me those questions. I don't know what you're talking about, neither do I know who brought you here and for what reason. My job is to let you go. I don't know what you did, and I don't want to know. Do you understand me?"

"No, madam, I don't understand the logic behind this. Are you telling me that you can kill and release people at will in this country? Is this what is happening in all prisons in Juba? I mean, I have heard of this before and now I am an eyewitness. Then where are we going, madam? Is this the freedom my late brother and many other brothers and sisters died for? I thought we have a country where matters are taken care of maturely, but now I confirm we don't. I want those who brought me here. I want them to tell me what crime I have committed. I was almost killed by those bandits and they then came to rescue me and others only to single out the two of us. We are victims of both the government and the bandits. Now, where is Yien, the other young man who came with me? I never seen him for the other two weeks!"

"Calm down, Mr. Peter. You're talking too loud. I am trying to help you. Do you not understand? They can kill you and no one else will know about it. Let me ask you a question. Have anyone ever come here to visit you since you came?" she asked, looking at me right in the eyes. I could see she was already heart-broken. Before long, tears ran down both her right and left cheeks. Words were difficult to come out.

"You're my son's age mate, and I don't want you to die!" she whispered into my left ear before falling on me full weight. I could feel a motherly love for the first time again in over twenty years.

"I hate my job! They once forced me to sentence my son to death for a crime he didn't commit. Please, go now! I don't want you to die!" she lamented with her tears raining on my bare back. "Shut up! You're indeed a woman! Who taught you to speak such things against your own law? You must face the law today yourself. Leave him alone!" an unfamiliar voice shouted from a distance. I didn't even know how he could see or hear us when I couldn't even see him. She was still shivering and almost wailing. She was holding me firmly. But will they hang her because of me? Is it not a crime to hang her? I was thinking.

"You can go. But please, let them kill me instead. I am a man and you are but a woman, a mother. You've not committed any crime. Is it a crime to tell the truth in this country or, rather, in this world? Please, go. Go to him, mom!" I spoke out as loud as I could. And there she was going to the officer with higher ranks than herself.

"Brother. You don't ask them questions. All you need is to leave as soon as possible. I have seen them shoot a man in the head for speaking in his native language when he was told not to do so. The man was like telling them he had the right to speak in his language at least to those who can understand that language. But unfortunately, they instantly shot him dead. You've caused trouble to both you and that kind old woman. Can't you hear? They are now beating her up! She might lose her job as a result!" the other familiar man but still nameless was speaking to me now. "But who's behind all this brutality? Is it the government or some individuals? Does the president even know what these people are doing in our prisons? Do the members of parliament know what's happening here each and every day? Let me tell you, Mr. policeman. My elder brother died to liberate this country from the Arabs during the Nasir Battle of 1989. I am not a foreigner or a second class citizen. I can now speak up even if it means death. I don't care what the thieves will do to me. In fact, I want to be heard. I want the head of the state to hear this crime in prisons!"

"Listen, Mut. How are you going to do this? You're now a prisoner. You're going to let them kill both you and us! Do you understand your actions? Don't you hear her screaming? They are hitting her with their hands and with their gun barrels right now. They even stepped on her neck with those boots. She's dying all because of your mistake!" he shouted.

Indeed, how will I even reach to the president before they do away with me? Even if I could shout to the top of voice, will the president hear me from this cell? Even if some passers hear me shout or wail, will they know what's happening inside here?

"Now get back to the cell!" he shouted at me for the first time. I had to get in as he closed the iron door behind me and I could hear the click of the lock as it does what it was created to do. Am I wise enough? Why did I do this to myself and to that poor woman? Maybe she's already dead by now. Why do these innocent people work in this dangerous place? Do they work here merely because of money or are they fearing for their own lives?

I was now back into my cell. This was the world only me and little creatures lived. These creatures seemed to have developed a friendship with me. These were bedbugs, fleas, mosquitos, spiders, and lies. One of the spiders was so special. It seemed to be feeling sorry for me each time it sneaked into my cell. It could stare at me for a very long time before making those twists and turns as if to show the discomfort.

But the mosquitoes didn't care. They tried their best to always keep me awake. Bedbugs could feed on me regardless of being at night or day. They feasted as long as they were hungry. That was how we related. Even the heat was not enough to prevent sleep. One can't differentiate the night from the day. All was darkness. I could hardly read my Bible or sing from the hymnal. The books were also suffering from my sweat. The smell of my own urine and faeces was no longer an issue. Insanity is just a different mentality. Every human is insane but in a different level. Even those you see on our streets who pick up rubbish and smile at it are perfectly at peace. At least they are free. Life is all about freedom. But what freedom did we fight for? Why are the children and the wives of the deceased suffering in our country? Why are their names not found in any pay list?

"Come out!" he shouted as he pushed the key through a hole in the padlock behind the door before pulling the door wide open. Before I knew it, the same dark clothe was now on my both eyes and he tied it behind my head. I could tell he was tying my hands. Then he was tying my legs together but not too tight. My hands were tied together in front of me, not backwards as of before.

"Maybe this is good news? Are they taking me into another cell? Are they going to dump me into the Nile River? I don't know what's going on right now."

Then I could tell that the two men were now carrying me out of the cell and I could feel we were in an open space. This might have been the middle of the compound. Then they put me in something like a metal box. No, it was a military pickup! We now moved out of the fence and I could see it was clicking to a closing point as we departed.

"Maybe I am dead? But I am alive still."

After passing through many twists and turns, we then arrived somewhere that was cooler than ever. Then the car stopped and then the men picked me up and put me down only for them to start the car and then they started to leave me alone. The night was so dark that I could sense it. You could hear the silence. "Where exactly is here? Oh, I can hear someone speak. This must be a marketplace!" I thought to myself. "Inta munu?" a male voice asked. He sounded to be scared and wanting to retreat. I was much more scared than him and this made me take time to respond. Fear is a reality. But at least I was feeling some kind of relief and freedom from the prison's oppression. I had to respond to him, anyway.

"Mut. Please, help me!"

"But who are you?" he asked again. Then the other people began to come to the scene. "These must be shopkeepers or other kidnappers?" I thought. "Please remove these ropes first and I will tell you who I am and where I am from," I said as the men came closer. Some were still scared and they were keeping their distance. But this one man took the risk. After removing the veil, I could see that this was the Konyo-konyo market. Then he untied my hands and legs and looked at me in a surprise. He could sense my innocence. I still found it harder to stand, let alone walking. I was suffering. As the morning fully came, I then knew the exact place where I was. But I had no transport money. I needed help. I couldn't walk home alone.

CHAPTER 24

June 6th 2011, Bor, South Sudan

"Can you remember all our leaders from the first liberation struggle to the current ones?" I asked. The old man had to prepare his mind before answering any of my questions. Was he concerned why I was asking him those questions almost on a daily basis? I didn't know the answers.

"No, this isn't possible. But I can tell you what I can remember. Remembering things from one's head is not a sign of intelligence or education, is it? I think most of you these days don't know what knowledge is. Whenever you go to school, they want you to report back to the teacher everything you have ever learned almost word-per-word. But this is unfair!" he shouted.

"You're right, grandpa. I've read something like that about an American businessman who was asked to mention or describe things in their history. But he told the person questioning him that this is foolish. Education is not all about the accumulation of useless knowledge. Rather, it's about actionable knowledge."

"Good. This means you're thinking now. To answer your question. I remember several of our leaders from 1955 to date. But I don't know many of them, simply because I never heard of them, let alone meeting them in person. It's not easy to meet your leaders nowadays, is it? Do you know all our current leaders in person?" he asked, looking at me now.

"No, I don't know all of them."

"That's true again. Why do you want me to remember all our leaders from the first liberation struggle to the current ones?"

"I am asking because I want to know if I may also know them all or not. The reason is mainly for our historical records. Many of you who were there in the army are dying, each year. This means our history is also dying. Before you die, you can tell me what you know and this is the driving force behind."

"Okay. I will then tell you what I know if this is the sole purpose for your questions," he agreed.

"From 1955, I can recall leaders from both Sudans, the north and the South. From the south, I remember those of Akuot Atem, Kuany Latjor, Emilio Taffeng, Aggrey Jaden, Gordon Muortat Mayen, Joseph Lagu, Dr. Garang de Mabior, Dr. Lem Akol, Kerubino Kuanyin, Samuel Gach Tut, Dr. Riek Machar, Cdr. Salva Kiir, and many others."

"Great. I am glad that I know some of these people in person. Most of them died before our independence but we still celebrate them each year. Now, what do you think these people will say if they happen to resurrect from their graves? Do you think they will be happy with the current affairs in our new country? Do you think they will regret fighting for us with their lives?"

"Well, each one of them will have his own feelings and reactions based on many different factors. But I think most, if not all of them, will be disappointed in some degrees. This is because this is not what we fought for. Look, even we who are alive now, none of us is happy about what's happening in our country."

"That means you're not happy?"

"Sure! I am not happy because we don't have a good governing system yet. Do you know that most of the veterans are forgotten already whether dead or alive? I am sure you know that our army is the only suffering army on earth because they either don't receive enough salary, or it never comes. Think about that. These are men and women with families to feed and children to take to the best schools."

"I see. But is the problem with the top leadership or is it with those tasked to do this?"

"It's from every level. Even the top leadership is corrupt. Then every step downward is also corrupt. This however is not only in South Sudan. You can find corruption in every country, but in a different way, my son. For us, we steal money and then take it outside the country to invest it there. In Kenya, they do the opposite. They steal the money and then use it to create jobs within the country, and this is a good way to steal because the investment comes back to the people of Kenya. For us, our leaders take their children to the best schools outside the country. And whenever they are sick, they also go outside. I don't know what will happen if the foreign hospitals will refuse to treat them one day. I don't know what will happen if the travel will be restricted for whatever reasons. Maybe our leaders will die?"

"I do believe every developed and every developing country started from where we are right now before they became what they are today. For this reason, I still believe we will catch up with the rest of the world, but after some time. What do you think?"

"You're right again, son. But we don't have to learn the hardest way. The countries you're talking about now took many years to reach to the level they are in now because of many factors, including but not limited to lack of technology in those days, and also lack of education. But look at us. We got our independence at the time technology has advanced and education has reached its peak. How long do you think we'll keep waiting until we see development?"

"I can't tell how long we are going to wait. Maybe as long as I will be dead for a hundred years. But that's still a possibility. Time will come when the people of this country will no longer be judged based on their tribes but on their abilities, just as Martin Luther King Jr. said it many years ago about the American people. Many years later after he was killed, Obama ruled America for two terms. That was a fulfilled prophecy, wasn't it? My prophecies will also come into fulfilment even long after my death."

"But we want them to come into fulfilment when we are still alive and well. I want to enjoy the fruits of my labour. I and many others have been fighting for the independence of this country. Your Dr. Garang was not for it. He was for the unity of the Sudan and then he thought he would eventually become the president of the republic. Will the Arabs allow him to achieve that goal? They can't. And at the end, they dealt away with him miserably. This is what it means to be an Arab. Only the Israelites, their cousins, know them well."

"But today we are not under the Arabs, are we? And we're still facing the worse, right?"

"These are their disciples, my son. Look. You want them to come for my head! You can't talk negative about them and still live. They are beasts. Wild beasts in human clothing, my son. Don't let them know I am speaking against their *ruler-ship*. They're not leaders but rulers. Do you know how their vehicles run? Terror!" "I know. I know how they run in towns. Every other thing on the road must come into a standstill mode whenever they're passing by. This is the first sign that they don't care about their citizens. But as far as I know, they'll still pass on by all means. Then the time will come for other good leaders to lead the nation forward towards the development we're now talking about. Peace and reconciliation will finally come. Then our children will enjoy the fruits of our labour. We have to do our best and do it now."

"I thought all these good things would happen during our lifetime, but I was and I am still wrong. As you said, it'll take a very long time before we eat the fruits of the land. You know what natural resource we have apart from the oil revenues. We have the land. This land is the most fertile land of all lands on earth. We have water from rivers as well as from the skies above, each and every year. In the water, we have all kinds of fishes. On land, we have all kinds of wild animals, which will bring us wealth. In our swamps, we have all kinds of beautiful and useful creatures on earth. But are we going to enjoy all of that?"

"Yes, even if it's not going to be you and me, our great grandchildren will enjoy them, grandpa. Good enough you're still hear and enjoying your life. Many people of your age have passed on long ago. Most of them died in our bushes when they were fighting for our liberation. They never saw the end of it, but you did. For this reason, you can be thankful."

"Yes, and I am thankful for that. But I am not happy because of the everyday happenings in our country. Life is too hard as you might know. I am hearing about the new rebel groups as well as the killings of our innocent civilians on our roads. This is not what we fought for. Our liberators died in vain if this is the case. I think none of them can be happy now if they happen to come back to life."

"I agree with you, grandpa. But at least all of you have done your part. I have to do my part, too. My part is to educate as many people as I can. This is why I want to know our history from the people like you. I will then tell my children about how our country came into being. Isn't this part of your work?"

"You people are always talking about the government. You're going to face it rough! Why don't you talk about the Dinka and the other tribes who are always preparing to attack us and raid our livestock?" she questioned.

"Leave us alone! This grandson of yours is mad. But I enjoy his talks. He's my kind. He's my blood. He thinks in the same way, just as I do. But you don't think in the same way, do you?"

"No, I can't think like that. I am wise. I must be careful, especially in a country like ours where we're never free to speak out our minds. Even those lizards may listen and report you to them in Juba. Don't you know that ether can take messages to other people at the other end of the globe? Therefore, nothing is hidden in the face of the earth. Nothing is unknown!" she concluded.

"Grandma. I understand your concerns. All I want to know is how many leaders we had from the first liberation struggle to date. Then we ended up talking about the current leaders, which is not too bad, is it?"

"It's bad because of your own safety. I am not saying that you should not ask questions but that you must stay within the topic. I have heard that people were arrested, never to be seen again. These leaders are killers, and they don't care about elders or youngsters. They can kill at will. Do you know this?" she asked again, now looking at me in the eyes.

I understood her. She was right in every way. All humans don't see things in the same way. Even colours seem to look slightly different for women then they do for men. I am not sure if this is an unconfirmed theory or not. I was told women see the slightest differences in colours more than men. I was also informed that women have a better sense of smell then men do. This is why they detect danger faster and then act. They scream as loud as possible.

CHAPTER 25

December 15th 2013, Juba

"Do you know what is happening now in your capital city?" a brother from Canada was calling me at 4a.m asking me about my capital city.

"Well, I have been hearing gunfire since 10p.m yesterday until now, but I can't tell what's going on. Whenever I try to call other people here in Juba, our local network seems to be on strike. There is no success in communication."

"Okay. I am calling to let you know that the yesterday's meeting at the Nyukuran Cultural Centre has given birth to the gunfire you are now hearing. He's started it again like that of 1991. Please, don't go out of the compound until further notice. They are already targeting people like you with marks on the foreheads. They won't know you are not one of the rebels. Do you understand me?"

"Yes, brother, I do understand very well. Thank you very much for the information. Imagine, I live in this city but I barely know what's happening here."

"It's okay. You people are still in the dark. Bye for now!" he said and then hanged out.

"Who's that?" asked my wife.

"It's one of our brothers from the diaspora. He's saying that there is a serious fighting outside and that people like me must be careful not to walk freely in the city as usual. This is too bad to hear. Those people outside our country seem to know a lot of things about this country more than we do."

"I can't stay here, no matter what. I must go to our state and then die with our people. I have no mother or relatives in this town. If you have, I will leave you with them. I am going to the Upper Nile region!" she shouted. But before long, a shell landed on our backyard, making the concrete building shake like a piece of paper. At least we had to listen to that.

I was still trying to call different people from different sides of the city, but the phones were not going through. The network itself seems to have been cut off. This is too much. It doesn't say anything. It doesn't say whether the phones were off or if they were out of network. Whenever I tried to dial any numbers, it seemed someone is pressing the end call key all the time. Something must be terribly wrong.

I guess the government didn't want anyone to talk. They didn't want people to communicate with each other. Communication may be dangerous to both the government and the rebels, if there were any rebels as such. I didn't know what to say or do.

"We came here in order to go to the Upper Nile region. None of us knew beforehand that this is what is going to happen. I think you can also hear the gunfire from the outside. It's also dark still. It's about four in the morning. We'll have to check out tomorrow if at all planes are still traveling to our region. But we can't tell at the moment."

"I don't care whether there're planes or not. I must go. I can't die here alone. You know very well that your father is in the Upper Nile. All our parents and relatives are there. We must go there and die together with them!"

"Whether it means to die or to live with them, this is not my concern at the moment. What I am concerned about is our lives. Listen, they're still fighting against each other just from the outside. I can't tell if we're going to make it to the next morning let alone to the Upper Nile. Do you hear the bombs and the artilleries?"

"I am hearing everything. But this is none of my business. I must leave this place as soon as daybreak. I don't belong here. I belong to the Upper Nile."

"None of us was born in Juba. Do you understand my points? No one said we're not going to the Upper Nile region. We're here for that very reason. We left Yei to the far west just to go to the Upper Nile to see our parents and relatives. But now the war is breaking out. I am sure if this is a quo, then it will happen everywhere where there is an army barrack. This of course includes our Upper Nile region. If this happens, we better go back to Yei and wait until further notice. I think Yei will be more secure, at least for some time. Then when things are back to normal, we can come back and proceed to the Upper Nile. Is that okay with you?"

"Didn't I know what you're going to say before you even open your mouth to say it? I knew you're coward! You're already running away in your mind. I am better than you even though I am but a woman. I can defend myself and my people against the enemy. I know that from all sides our enemies will rise to crush our elders and young people in a few days. Now, what kind of a man are you if you can't go and die with your people? Instead, you want to go and hide?"

"I have been fighting the real war for the independence of our country. But what's going on right now is purely for a seat. They're fighting over the presidential seat. They're not fighting for something good. In fact, it's a foolish war if you can allow me to say that. I am not refusing to go. But remember, all the airliners will not be allowed to travel as soon as today until further notice. You think you know what you're talking about but you don't. I am a man. I know what it means to have a quo in a country like South Sudan."

"You're not a real man. Real men are brave and could fight to the last bullet. Real men worry about their people and their land. I am better than you though I am but a woman. I must go and die with our people in the Upper Nile region. I love my parents. I love my people more than you do."

"It's okay if you think I am not a real man. That doesn't make me what you think I am in any way. I know who I am. I don't need any other person's approval of me. The issue is not about me but about the situation we're in. Please, calm down. I know you have a point to make. But may you also listen to other people's points of view?"

It was now in the morning and I could hear the gunshots just around the compound. The fighting was still going on almost everywhere. But Rockcity was much better than that side of the Newsite and Bilpham. The fighting broke out around 10p.m at Giyada, the main military barrack in the city. It was between the presidential guards. Conflicting reports began to sprung up shortly after, mostly verbal, and this was how we humans have been communicating ever since. Rumours are more than realities.

"Yes, uncle, can you hear me now?"

"Yes, I can hear you. We're fucking your maternal uncles. Wait a minute, I'll call you back later," he said as he pressed on the end call button and fired his gun thrice in a row. I could hear the gunfire again and again. Sad indeed. They were killing themselves by now. I just don't know when this kind of hatred between these brother-tribes was going to come to an end. Their language tells the world that they might have come from the same great grandparents, yet they hated themselves to hell. They could fight to the last bullet, killing each other with no mercy at all. Oh, God, bless them!

"Hello, uncle, can you hear me?" I was now trying my best to speak to my other uncle on the other side of the fight. He was not speaking even though the phone was counting down, meaning he's accepted my call. "Yes, nephew. I can hear you loud and clear. We're busy, fucking the rest of your fraternal uncles. They think they can overrun us because they are as many as husks of the grain, but we are few and more brave and powerful than they think. Soon, we'll capture this city and declare ourselves rulers. Wait! He's aiming at me!" and off goes the phone on his end. I could hear the shouts of victory and the gunfire was like a disco as they called it.

At that point, who was fucking who? Who were chasing who? I can't tell. It didn't matter who was winning the battle. It didn't even matter to me who was going to win the war at large. I don't have sides. They're all my uncles as they rightly kept saying to me over the phone. The same thing happened to many more nationals. They come from both sides. They belong to both the warring tribes. Indeed, the political disagreement or misunderstanding as they soon will call it, became a tribal issue in a matter of one hour. This is the same everywhere in Africa. This is the same thing everywhere on earth. I had to pray and kept praying for the two tribes. Yes, all tribes have their own issues, but since these are the major tribes in the country, their clash always means too much suffering and the death of thousands.

Look, we've died much during the national war for the whole of Sudan. Today, we're dying for our own war of leadership. What's in the leadership seat that's much better than the lives of our people?

"What have you been talking about the whole night?" my fraternal uncle asked. He wanted to know why we have been arguing at night.

"Your daughter is too young. This generation of yours in so immoral! For us, we don't bother our wives until the child is three years old," he went on.

"No, uncle. It's not about such issues. My wife says we have to go to the Upper Nile. I am going out now to look for a plane ticket from the airport."

"Is your wife normal? Are you both mad? Can't you hear the gunfire? Let me tell you. I just came back from the airport because your uncle's wife wants to travel to the Upper Nile as well, but none of the airlines is operating until further notice. And, please, never try to enter the road. They're hunting for people with those marks. Even here, six soldiers came this morning, ridding on a bodaboda, looking for people from house to house. Haven't you seen them? I am concerned about you now. Please, don't allow her to drive you out into the streets!" he commanded.

But I had to go to town. She was pressing on. She can't give up even after our uncle spoke to me in her presence. I had to go to the airport. On my way, I could see this guy, pointing at me with that short black riffle.

"*Eeŋa kɔɔr bä moc muony?*" I was asking the same man. Then with a surprise, he asked me to leave quickly. He wanted to shoot me dead but I spoke to him in his language. Arriving at the airport after some long distance of footing, I could see that there were no planes flying into the Upper Nile's Malakal airport. The fighting had already spread to Bor, the capital of the Jonglei State and also in some parts of the Upper State such as Kokpiot, the military training centre.

I had to go back home, but the road was blocked. No vehicles allowed and I had to walk footing. Soldiers were scattered everywhere on our national capital streets to patrol it. They may shoot at will. But I had to do my best. I loved her so much.

CHAPTER 26

July 16th 2015, Yambio

"What can you say about the South Sudanese?"

"I think they are the most joyful people on the planet. No matter what happens to them, they endure it. These are sheep, but their leaders are wolves in sheep's clothing," he went on. I didn't know if this included him since he was one of those leaders.

"What do you mean?"

"I mean what I am saying, my son. Our leaders have failed us and I am sure you know this. Why could we still fight and kill each other in this country if it's not because of our leaders?" he asked, looking at me in the eyes. I didn't know what was going on in his heart.

"I think our leaders are a part of the whole issue. I don't think they're the cause of every criminal activity in the country. Look, thieves are from every tribe. A thief from Nuer can steal and kill people. He can kill the Nuer or the Dinka. He can steal cows, women, children, and whatever he wants from any community. In the same way, a thief from the Dinka can do the same things. Now, can we blame our leaders for this?"

"Leadership is everything, my son. By now, if we do have a government, our civilians couldn't have those dangerous guns in their hands. But they do so to protect themselves from other harmful neighbouring tribes who always want to revenge on them. How long will it take for our government to be able to protect our people? Why are our people the ones to protect themselves?" he went on.

"I think if our people love each other and if they could stop those inter-communal attacks, there will be no fear. There will be peace and harmony among our people. What do you think?"

"Humans are animals. Nothing else. If you don't treat them as such, and make laws that must be kept, they can do whatever evil they want to do. This is what's happening in our country today. Too much freedom is deadly. If I can ask you. Where do you think our civilians get their guns from?" he asked.

"I think they buy them from our own soldiers?"

"It's not a question. It's a reality. They buy guns with their cows. They sell their belongings in order to buy those them arms from our armed forces who are not being paid as they have to. If their salaries come on time, and it's enough, do you think they will sell their guns? If one sells a gun and he or she is punished by law, do you think anyone will do the same thing again?" he questioned.

"I have no evidence of where they buy guns from. How do you know they buy guns from our armed forces in this country?" I was asking him, looking at him in the eyes as if to discern his feelings through the heart's window, the eyes. Our human eyes tell the world what we're thinking and feeling, no matter how we try to fake it. He understands my gestures, too.

"I also agree with that. Looking for such evidence is like an atheist looking for the evidence of God's existence when he or she is the evidence. Pure ignorance. In the same way, you know very well that I am not lying. The evidence is known even to a five-year-old kid. You must also know the evidence."

"I have heard the president of the republic saying the same thing. But he never said where the civilians buy their guns from. All he said was that they buy them to protect themselves. He also said a thief can come from anywhere."

"Because we have the evidence, we know where they're buying them from. I know people who bought guns by name. We've been buying and selling arms ever since before our own independence. It's not a new practice, son. Even in the United States of America, people who are not even in the army buy guns to use them at will. They can use them to learn how to shoot a target. I know all these things."

"But for us, we use them to shoot and to kill each other. We use them to show that we're much more important than others. We use them to raid our very own villages. Do you think kinship concept is the real deal here? Do people raid and kill each other because they think those people are good as dead? What can you say about the inter-communal violence?"

"I think there're many causes to both the communal and the inter-communal violence. When thieves go to steal, they must kill the owners of the cattle before they take it. This creates conflict between the people. It would have been much better if they only take the cattle without killing the people. But this can't happen all the time for many good reasons. If the owners see the raiders, he or she must do something about it, thus, ending up being killed. He or she can even kill one or some of the raiders, depending on the situation."

"And over the years, hatred built up between the people groups, is that what you're saying?"

"Yes, that's correct. It then became an enmity between the tribes which are close to each other. But some tribes such as Murle can travel many miles away from their homeland to do just that. They can raid cattle and abduct children. They have been doing this for centuries. There're lots of evidence for this."

"So, whenever a Dinka or Nuer sees a Murle, he remembers everything about these people, even if this is not one of the thieves?" I asked. "That's true. I don't think anyone accepts the fact that there're no thieves in the Murle community. We believe all of them are but terrible thieves because our history proves it. It's not a theory. It's an evidence and you can't deny this unless you're an atheist who is always in search of what he's holding in his hands. That's akin to madness, isn't it?"

"Yet, it's a fact that not all Murle are thieves?"

"Yes, it's also true. But you can't convince others to believe in that truth. You know that it's true but not everyone knows or accepts the same thing. In fact, many of our people will argue with you based on their inherited knowledge. This is why we still hate ourselves as tribes in this country even in the 21st century. We believe what we have been told whether it's true or not."

"But do you believe we're the most joyful people on earth as you have just said earlier?"

"Yes, because we're the most ignorant, we're the most joyous people on earth. We die for those useless courses, and yet we celebrate. Whenever we hear that a Dinka have died, we jump up with joy. When a Dinka hears that a Nuer have died, he celebrates the death of his perceived enemy. But are we enemies? Who says we are enemies to each other? Even when there's a serious famine, we still believe in God to help us, and He does, always. This is resilience. This is a very good thing. Natural disasters do occur everywhere on the planet, and this doesn't mean the world has come to an end, does it? Even in America, people are dying of unknown sicknesses and diseases. New diseases are coming up every generation, and we don't know what to do with them. Yet, South Sudan trusts in God in all things. This makes us the most joyful people on the planet."

"You mean ignorance is joyful?"

"Yes, and it is going to be. Think about it this way. Many years ago, we didn't know much about Malaria, even though it was there. We used to call it, *Lerakɔɔn*. It doesn't kill anyone in those days. But when they began to name it and talked about it too much, Malaria became deadly. Your thoughts can make you sickly, or they can heal you, depending on what they are. Because people worry too much about their health nowadays, they become frequently sick. Because people know about those tiny little germs, they are suspicious all the time that they'll get infected. We used to drink dirty water with no ill health, but try to do that today and tell me what will happen to you. Your mind is always infected."

I think he's right. Nowadays, people get sick almost as soon as they finish their treatment. Sickness becomes the order of life. People seem to also know what they are suffering from. Any kind of ailment must be treated with an injection. The antibiotics are overused. They're mostly used for the wrong kinds of sicknesses. Not every headache and body pain is caused by Malaria or Typhoid. I think the old man was very right. Our minds make us sick. We overthink sickness even when we might only be facing some simple kinds of ailments in our bodies. But how can we help our people from this madness? They think they know what they are suffering from. Will they listen to us?

"You're right. But is that not an insult?"

"It may sound like an insult. But if it's an insult at all, I am insulting myself. Whether we're insulting other tribes or our leaders, we're insulting ourselves because our identity is South Sudan. But do you think this is an insult?"

"I agree with you about the mind. People overthink and they end up becoming sickly, almost all the time. This is indeed a result of too much wrong information and wrong knowledge or education. But to conclude that all of us are like this is an insult. What do you think?"

"Each country has a mastermind. This is the common thinking pattern that affects everyone living in that country. This is why all foreigners in our country watch their media while they're here. We rarely do the same whenever we're outside the country. Even in Juba, do you think we listen or watch our very own SSBC news?" he asked, turning his attention to those flying goose overhead. His love for wildlife is what I have inherited. Be loved nature and the animals in it. He loved birds, plants, fishes, amphibians, reptiles, humans, and everything else in nature. He loved the nonliving things as well.

"What do you mean by a mastermind?"

"I meant to say that there is a mind that's common to many people without their knowledge. In this case, we in this country don't believe in ourselves as we should. We have the highest rate of illiteracy in the world. Try to text your friends and see by yourself how many of them will respond to your texts. Even those of us who know how to read don't practice reading much. Simple things such as women's and girls' issues still kill many of us each year. A young man wants to hang out with your sister, but if he ever finds you with his sister in a secluded place, you'll face him that day. Sad."

"What's the solution?"

"True education, not schooling, plus true knowledge and the fear of God. These are the only solutions I know. Education is more than reading and writing in any human language. The fear of God means reverential fear, which is out of love, based on how we know Him, personally.

CHAPTER 27

November 28th 2020, Loki, Kenya

"Were you here in 2005?"

"Yes, I was here. But I was only 6 years old that year," explained the young man. He was no longer a child after those fifteen years have passed by. He was now 21 and working at one of the best hotels in the area called Makuti.

"I was here in 2005 as a theology student with Middle East Reformed Fellowship, MERF. I guess their compound lies west of this place, if I am not wrong."

"No, you're not wrong. You still remember the place quiet well. The airstrip is now southwest of here. It's just a few minutes' walk from this guesthouse," he explained. I was now thinking about how years fly away. I was now 37. I was 22 when I first landed in Lokichoggio, Kenya, from Abwong, Upper Nile, South Sudan. But how come that this place was no longer our border in the year 2020, just fifteen years later? I was told that the Sudanese border with Kenya was Lodwar in those olden days, but this is another hot cake for now. I had to keep these thoughts to myself. I had to tell myself, "You have to believe you're now in Kenya, anyway." We've our own issues to face, not border issues. None of our borders was correct. Even our border with the Sudan was not demarcated. It was still unknown even though everyone knew where the real border was. Don't even talk about our border with Ethiopia, Uganda, Congo, and the Central Africa Republic. We still had a long way to go.

Do we even have our airspace in our hands? Not at all. It wasn't so at the time. But we were a country with a government and people. We have the land and its natural resources. We have plants, animals, birds, and fishes. We have plenty of water everywhere.

After passing through other road blocks from Nadapal to Loki, I was now going through another one before reaching to the Kakuma Refugee Camp. The camp was known as Kalebeyei.

"Is there any Sudanese in here?" asked the policeman more than five times. He was doing this while looking at us on the small car and everyone was silent. I was the only South Sudanese. I didn't like the name, "Sudanese," because in my mind, I was not a Sudanese. I was a South Sudanese, a very different country. I don't know how long will it take for the world to acknowledge the truth.

"Yes, I am here!" I responded after being irritated.

"Come here!" he commanded. He literally refused to take my ID, my passport, even though I was giving it to him. He was insisting I come out of the car and follow him into a small structure on the roadside. Coming there, he was looking at me in the eyes, and I was doing the same thing. I was wondering what crime have I committed that deserved being taken aside. He can simply look at my passport and see if my visa was valid just as other police officers have done it all along.

"What's the primary reason for you to come to Kenya?" he asked, still looking directly into my eyes.

"I am here for a visit. I'll be back to my country as soon as possible."

"Give me 10k Kenyan money," he said, now looking away from my face. I was getting annoyed at this point, and I was studying him from the toes to the hair on his head. From the sole of his feet to the crown of his head, I was interpreting his actions and emotions.

"Sir. Look at me now. Why do I have to give you $100 dollars?" I questioned him.

"Because you are traveling at a wrong time."

"Do you mean people are not traveling?"

Yes, people are not traveling, and you know this. Don't tell me you don't know about COVID-19."

"But I am coming with other Kenyans who're doing business in South Sudan. Why did they even allow us to leave South Sudan? Why did they give me an entry visa into Kenya if people are not traveling?"

"Do you think this is your violent country?" asked another policeman on casual clothing, not on uniforms. He was standing behind me. I was angered and I didn't even see or care about what they were saying about me or to me. This is serious. They were trying their best to rob me. They were robbers, not security personnel.

"Sorry. What did you just say?" I asked.

"Do you know that there's something cooking at the border?" the first policeman asked. He was doing this to turn my attention away from the other police officer who stepped too much into the issue. He knew I was angry, ready for anything they wanted.

"I don't know about the border issues between Kenya and South Sudan, and I don't want to know about it because it's none of my business. Are you telling me that South Sudan and Kenya are no friends anymore? Are you declaring war against us? But why are you not clear about it? Let me tell you. It's better to talk about war with us than when it's a reality. I am sure you will not talk about it if it is going to happen. Don't remind me of war. I know what it means to be in war and I can't say you will soon have your own civil war in Kenya because this is bad. I am speaking to you like a Kenyan national. Because there's peace in Kenya, I am happy and I can't wish you war. But please, never remind us of our violence. Any country can end up in violence. Look, when you fought in 2007, did you go and hire South Sudanese to come and fight? Was it not real Kenyans fighting?" I lectured him. He was now looking at me in the eyes. I didn't know what he was thinking about right. Maybe he was planning to attack me? I didn't know. But I was ready for anything. They were making me angry. They were doing it intentionally so that can I do something foolish so that they will arrest me for it and then ask my family and friends to vail me out with a huge amount of money. I knew this because they have been doing this very thing to many South Sudanese before me. They were used to robbery.

"Why do you speak like this?" he asked.

"I am angry with you, sir. Are you here to cause issues between the two countries? I am ready to go to the county government and report you because you are robbers. Are you doing your job? What if I give you 100k now, will you not allow me to enter the country even if I don't have valid traveling documents? What if I am a COVID-19 positive, and I hand you the money, will you not allow me to enter the country? You mean you don't care about Kenyans? What if I am a terrorist and I pay you money, will you allow me in? I am asking you. Sir, you're behind the news. Don't call us Sudanese. Sudanese are Arabs, but do I look like one? You and me look almost exactly the same. The reason why we fought against the Arabs for years was because we are Africans like you. You're my brothers but do you know this fact? If I happen to go to Sudan, they'll mistreat me more than you're doing to me right now, all because they think I am not one of them, and I am not. Do you know our history? Do you know what role you Kenyans played in our liberation struggle? I am talking to you! Why do you keep embarrassing us on your roads? Even in my county, I can't be happy if they embarrass Kenyans in my presence. This is because we're brothers. We're true Africans!"

"Who is embarrassing you?" he asked calmly.

"You, the Kenyan government!" I said. "Do you know what it means to be embarrassed?" he asked after a loud laughter. He was then motioning me to leave for the car, which was now far away on the roadside to the right hand side. "No, let him go back to his country!" shouted the other policeman. I could tell he was from Turkana because he resembled me almost in everything.

"My brother. Do you really have an issue with me? Look at you and then look at me. Why are you saying this? I am very ready to be exported if at all it's according to the law of this country. I want the world to hear today that Kenya doesn't want South Sudanese in her soil. Do you know how many

Kenyans are in South Sudan? Do you know how many South Sudanese are in Kenya? Go ahead and deport me right now. I am ready to go. This world is a world of technology. You never know if I am recording everything live. You can do whatever you want to do to me, and do it right now without any hesitation, but the whole world will hear about it in minutes. Don't ever incite us into anger for whatever reasons. We don't just get annoyed for nothing."

"This man is out of his mind. Just go to the bus! We can do anything to you right now, and no one will know about it. Don't you know that you're the only Sudanese here?" asked the first policeman.

"Sir, I am speaking on behalf of all South Sudanese. I am sure you don't care about the people. Imagine, if I only have 10k of the Kenya money right now and I give it to you, how will I continue with the journey ahead? Do you care about me?"

"Just go!" he commanded, pushing me away.

I had to leave. But I was still annoyed. I was angry. Entering the bus, everyone was waiting for me in a deep silence. This seemed none of them was happy with the police officers on the roadside.

"Did you give them money?" asked the Turkana driver. He looked sad. He tried to help me but they almost beat him up. "Money! I don't have money, my brother. But in every neighbouring country, people think that whenever they see a South Sudanese, they see the American dollars. What a foolish mind-set? We're not Americans! How can we have American dollars all the time? Even here in Kenya, does everyone have a lot of money?" I asked.

"Not all Kenyans think like this, my brother. But I understand. You have done well by not giving them even 1 shilling. These are thieves. They're taking a lot of money from your people, especially from those who don't have travelling documents. Even if they have valid visas, they still ask them to pay money."

"True. They asked me to give them money even though I have a valid visa, Yellow Fever Card, and a COVID-19 negative results test. All these documents are valid. I just got my visa in less than a day ago from Nadapal. My COVID-19 test is less than two days' old, which means it is still valid. This is sad!"

"Look, these brown guys are destroying our business. Because they kept doing this to you, we're facing the same when we go to your country. Sometimes, your government officials travel like normal citizens just to see what's happening on the roads. When they return to your country, they enforce the same habits. We need this to stop. This is just their nature," he explained.

CHAPTER 28

July 16th 2017, Abwong, South Sudan

"Do you think Sudan will one day reunite?"

"If South Sudanese are going to hate themselves for too long, yes. Nothing is impossible. Have you heard the saying, *"Anina sha'ab wahid fii dowlatein*? It means to say, 'we're one people in two countries.' The Arabs and the English people could never live in peace in one country, and this is what your country is all about. Those who lived deep in the villages were influenced by the white man, who used to drop them food from the skies. But those who lived in towns were under the Arabs. This is your New Sudan!"

"What do you mean?"

"I mean to say that our people think differently, simply because of the influences they got themselves into in their young ages. For those living in the far north, Arabs and their cultures are everything. Their food and clothes are always original. Nothing original comes from East Africa according to those who lived most of their lives with the Arabs. Also, for the same people, good life means being enslaved when your boss calls you a 'brother,' yet he uses you for his own good. Sitting and taking tea for the whole day without working for example is the culture of the north. For those of you who lived with the white man in the south, you see this as laziness, a bad habit. You were taught to work and not to beg or ask for help, or depend on others for almost everything. This is your country. This is a country divided by two different ideologies and cultures."

"But long before the *Kawajat* (white people) and the Arabs came, how was life in this country?"

"Life was different. We were truly African. This means a lot. We had our religious settings. We had our own technologies. We had our unique ideologies. In our world view, nothing like heaven or hell. God is in charge for both the good the evil. There's nothing called devil or Satan. This is because only God can bring both good and evil at will. He uses them for His own purposes. But today, we're told the Devil is a person," he explained with a deep smile.

"You mean those people living in the north are different people, and that there's nothing to unite us with them?" I asked. "Sure! They have their own ideologies, the Arab ideologies. Even a poor person in that country would love to sit while you work for him, so that he's seen as being a rich man. They're not hard-working people because of that ideology. They still want to have servants to serve them even in the 21st century. What a pity?" he asked.

"Are you telling me that the Arabs don't work?" I asked, looking at him with some seriousness. "Yes, they do work, but not as hard as you think. They use others to do the hard work for them, and they pay. They love using levers. They don't want to do the hard work themselves. The white man is very different. He wants to get himself dirty. That's why he has all the technology. But he lacks money. The Arabs are good with business. They buy and sell. They create wealth in a short period of time. They can start small and grow big. They're good with that. And you people are good with violence. Too much gossiping."

"Oh, okay! I thought you have just said we got all these things from the Arabs, didn't you?"

"Yes, you got laziness from the Arabs, and now it becomes yours. You own it. You love talking too much and work less. Even in your businesses and government offices, you take tea for the whole day and talk too much. You don't enjoy work. You enjoy luxury. You love pride. You don't know that pride comes with a price. But we were not like this."

"Do you think we're more like the Arabs today?"

"Yes, you are. You're even more than them. You've taking it to the next level. Look, our holidays are better called *waste-li-days*, and ask me why. Our people make sure a weekday is wasted, especially if the holiday falls on the weekends. They make sure they extend the holidays to the weekdays ahead. This is sad." He went on. I could see now that the old man was getting somehow stronger and stronger as we discussed these life issues. I can tell. He was annoyed. But is this not the same in every human generation? Humans seem to think back and regret about the new world that they're finding themselves into. They seem to prefer their past than their present or future, even if the past was as bad as today. This is something human. Well, even God seems to have His own regrets. He even regretted creating this sinful humankind.

"Why do you think Sudan will reunite?"

"I am not thinking it will. I was responding to your question. I don't know if it will reunite or not. But it's possible. It may reunite, if the south fails to be a country of its own. Also, Sudan is still having a lot of influence in our country. Everywhere you go, they still call you a Sudanese. Many of our people don't know the difference between Sudan and South Sudan. I wish we named our country something else with no Sudan in it. But will this change the mentality of both our people and our neighbours?"

"How does Sudan still influence us?"

"Don't you know that we have Sudanese in our presidency? Do we have members of parliament in their country? We don't. But we have advisors that are Sudanese in our government. Oh, we even have Kenyans and Nigerians, working in the highest government positions. Our personal ID cards are designed and printed by businessmen from either Kenya or Uganda. Even our military personnel have their IDs designed and printed by foreigners. How about our big men? They have their secretaries from foreign countries. Can't they find the same beautiful girls anywhere in this beautiful country? For this reason, we are being influenced by Sudan. All foods and clothes from Sudan are always the best. Many of us think it's even better to go back to Khartoum and confess we've made a BIG mistake to separate and become an independent state. They want us to say, '*Malish ya Bashir, anina ma gahasidiin*,' meaning to say, 'sorry Bashir, we never meant it.' This is a clue. The two sudans might reunite one day."

"What will happen if they reunite?"

"I think you will forever be a regretful piece of land on earth. You will forever be failures in the eyes of every nation. The Arabs will fuck both you and your wives in a broad daylight. They'll fuck your sons and daughters alike. That's a sad reality, my son. You'll be the talk of the day, all over the world. You'll be a people without vision. Those who died for this country will be dead in vain. I will forever be regretting in either my grave, or in heaven, or hell, depending on where I will be after death. But is there anything like heaven or hell?" he asked, looking at me in the eyes as if I had the answers. I was wondering about what he meant by the word, 'fuck,' and I didn't know if he was misusing it here. Maybe he was using it like the Americans do? Even in South Sudan, there're people who use the word to mean different kinds of things. For some, the word is an insult. For others, it's never meant to insult. I just hate the word.

"Is it possible to be free from both Arab and Western influence in South Sudan?"

"No. I don't think it's possible. The reason being that you're studying in their languages. Language is culture. Language is ideology. Language is identity. Look, nothing hates his language. Try to sound like a dog and see what will happen. Dogs will either get scared, or fall in love with you, just because language means identity. Everything has a language. There's even a universal language. No, it's not a sign language. It's a love language. Try to look at that lizard with a smile on your face and see how it will react to that gesture. He knows whether you mean it or you're faking it. As long as you abandon your African languages, you will always think, speak, and act like the Arabs, or like the Westerners. You will always have those foreign ideologies. Through technology, there's no way for the world to escape these Western ideologies" he went on. "Is it bad to have Western ideologies?" I asked. "Yes, and no. Yes, it's bad because no human culture or language is perfect. You know very well that even though the English language is the best, it is still limited in many ways. There're things you can't perfectly say in English, but you can in Nuer or Dinka. This means English is not the best language for everything. For example, the English word, 'chance,' is too negative when it forces you to believe and think that you're here by chance. No, it's not bad because it opens the world's eyes to small things such as disease-causing germs. Since most of the things were invented from the West, this is a good thing for the world. But I still suggest we take what's good from them and leave what is not."

"What else is bad from the West?"

"Individualism is as a selfish life. This is too bad for social animals like humans. It's good to discover yourself, but don't forget that you need others. No man is an isle land, right? This is a good saying from the West, too. Have time with yourself, but remember to socialise. This is good for your own life and health. You need people and the people need you. Take care of those relatives who can't care for themselves. It's a fulfilling career to help those in need, whether they're your relatives or not."

"Sure. But even in the West, I think people still care about other humans. This is why they're bringing us medicines and vaccines, what do you think? If the

Westerners don't care about other people, how can they even think of donating money and other tools and material things for us, here in Africa? Is it not a generalisation to think that Western people don't care or that they're all individualistic in their views?"

"I never said all of them are not caring. Don't forget that what they take out of Africa after that charity is what you can't even imagine with your small minds. They give because their people ask them to do so. They trust their men and women more than they trust you. They always have their own agendas. Most of them are either spies, or government security personnel. Some are journalists. Many of them are geologists, working under humanitarian organizations, or church missions. Watch out!"

"Is there anything else you want to say?"

"I have said it all. Sudan is a different country. It has different people. We're not one people in two different countries. Get that straight. If we're merely one people, then why did we fight for years? Do you think our heroes and heroines died in vain? We're truly African. God created people in their different races. The Sudanese are merely Arab, even though they're our cousins. Mark that well. We can't reunite!"

CHAPTER 29

March 19th 2020, Juba

"Have you heard about the new chemical warfare between China and the US?" she asked. Her eyes widened. My heart beat increased in each second.

"No, I never heard such as thing. What's going on? Are you talking about the economic war between those superpowers?"

"No! I am talking about the biological warfare, Mut. China created a virus to destroy America, but something went wrong in their laboratories before they could manage to carry out their attacks. Now, the virus is killing many people in China. Worse still, it's coming to Juba! We will soon die like flies, I tell you!" she exclaimed with fear visible in his eyes.

"I don't think you know what you're talking about, Aluel. I was told it's the other way around. I was informed that the Americans created the virus and then they sneaked it into China's Wuhan City to infect the Chinese. But the whole story changed. The virus is now destroying precious lives both in America and in China. It's even killing people worldwide."

"Do you all believe in those lies?" she asked.

"What lies?" Aluel asked with curiosity.

"Those lies you're talking about, Aluel. This virus was never created by any humans in any laboratory.

It's a direct punishment from God for the wickedness on earth. People are very wicked these days and God have seen this. How many prostitutes do we now have in Juba? How many are in Nairobi? Too many!"

"Nyaluak. I think you're almost right. But how do you know this is a punishment from God?" I was asking her while looking at her shinny hair. She was dark and slim. She was taller and beautiful to the eyes.

"I know because my pastor says so. He said these are happening as signs of the End Time. This means our Lord and Saviour will soon return and we will all be taken up into heaven!" she went on with some real excitement on her face. Her white and well-shaped teeth can tell what's happening inside her head.

"Oh, Nyaluak. Do you really believe in those tell tales? I better believe in Ngundeng tales or those of Dengdit and Nyikaango rather than their Western forms. They're mere human beliefs," Aluel objected.

"Okay, girls. Listen to me now. Whether the virus was created or whether it's from nature, what's the matter? What's wrong about that? Whether it's a punishment from God or gods, what's wrong with that? All I care about is if there's any cure for it. We can't prove whether it was created or it's natural. But we humans can learn how to fight against it. What are the ways given by the World Health Organisation so that people can either prevent or cure the disease?

Does any of you have any information about that? I just want to know how we can all deal with the disease. We don't have to point fingers either to other humans or to God or gods for that matter."

"Mut. You mean you trust in human solutions for this? This is done by the Devil. Satan is behind this. Have you not heard that they're closing churches and Mosques but they leave bars and disco places open? This is an attack on the religious centres. This is something spiritual. We have to fight it as such. No human-made medicine or vaccine will work perfectly. This is the work of the Devil!" Nyaluak went on.

"I think Mut is right. We need a human solution to this crisis. I don't think there's anything spiritual about it. We can't see or confirm if there is anything spiritual at all. Science can't either prove or disprove spiritual things. For this reason, we don't know if the spiritual world exists. Can we find out if there're medicines for the virus?" Aluel explained here part.

"You can tell us since you came up with the topic. Have you heard anything about the vaccines or medicines against it?"

"Because I think humans are not in control in this life, I don't think they can find any medicines or vaccines for this virus. It's not even a virus. It's a spirit. And for this reason, the best way to fight it and succeed is to fight it from its roots. This is why they're nasty and quick to close churches. The Devil knows very well that if we don't pray, he's going to win. Now, you already believe in the lie that this is a virus. I don't think it is a virus. It's the Devil!" Nyaluak explained.

"Aluel. Why do you think it's better to believe in Ngundeng instead of believing in the Bible or the Quran?" I asked, looking at her in the eyes.

"Mut. I think so because we're Africans. And to be frank, these are olden-day tell tales so to speak. They're outdated. These are Western traditions. If we have any reasons to still believe in those old-day tell tales, we already have plenty of them in our cultures. I have just given you a few examples."

"You don't believe in God?" Nyaluak asked.

"Is God a Christian?" Aluel asked.

"I think God is God. He's neither a Christian, nor a Muslim. He doesn't follow any religions of men, does He? I think He's everywhere, and He's for everyone. What do you girls think?"

"Exactly, Mut. You're a modern man. I love you!" Nyaluak answered, jumping and almost kissing my forehead in the process. She seemed to be overjoyed after my explanation.

"The Christian God is the only true God. The Bible tells us this truth, not me. Jesus said there's no other way to go to the Father except by Him. This means other religions and other gods are false. He's the way, the truth, and the life. We all must believe in Him in order to escape death in the lake of fire!" Nyaluak jumped in.

"Well, I have heard enough of that, Nyaluak. Every religion says the same things about themselves. Even in Christianity, some sect believes and teaches others that their church is the only one that's correct. This means the rest of churches are false and will all perish at the end of time. This to me is bullshit. How do they know their church is the right one out of hundreds of thousands of other churches in the world?" Aluel questioned.

"You, Dinka people. You don't believe in anything except your own ideas!" Nyaluak objected.

"No. I don't think it's about the Dinka or the Nuer. It's about those false beliefs, right?"

"Yes again, Mut. You're making me feel proud. You have just nailed it. It's not about the Dinka or the Nuer, neither is it about Shilluk, or Bari, or Maban. It's about these ancient beliefs and how they affect us today directly and indirectly. Nyaluak, it's about me. It's about what I believe in. It's about you, not the Nuer or the Dinka. Do you understand?" she asked. But Nyaluak seemed to be disturbed. She was not looking at any of us straight. She was looking away as if she was about to cry. I can understand a woman's heart. It's as soft as it is. It's a mother's heart whether she's still a child or a grownup. This heart gets offended as fast as possible. It gets hurt as quick as it can. But it's also a human heart. It can easily hurt other people's hearts as well.

"But it's true that you people never believe in other people's views. It's still my view that this disease is not human-made. It's a natural disease that came as a result of some spiritual forces behind it. For this reason, we humans can't either create or destroy it. Do you know that energy can neither be created nor destroyed?" Nyaluak explained.

"Yes, I can now agree with you, Nyaluak. If you know that it's natural, it means that it's not spiritual or supernatural. Is that okay? I never meant to attack you personally. I was only making my point as well. I do believe this was created, and if this is true, it can also be killed. Humans have learned how to cure diseases and this is done through science," Aluel explained her points again.

"You people are saying the same thing in your own unique ways. Whether we believe it's spiritual or not, the issue is about how to cure the disease. Whether we blame it on China, or America, all that is but an argument. We can't win any of that, can we? If not, then we need to think like humans, a family of a species. I believe in both science and God. This is because natural sciences prove the existence of God. Science and God are not enemies because they can both be studied in different ways. This is my belief."

"Mut. How do you reconcile the two worlds?" Aluel was now asking, looking at me in the eyes as if to prove me wrong. She was serious and I can tell. She purely believes in natural sciences. She doesn't seem to believe in the supernatural, whatsoever.

"I think I can help you before Mut answers your question. The simple answer is that you're the evidence of God's existence. Do you see this pen in my hands? The pen is the evidence that someone designed it. It didn't come into existence by chance unless chance means something else rather than what I know," Nyaluak explained.

"Well, I can see and feel myself. But can you see or feel God? This is the main issue here. I can study myself, but can I study God? This is my question, my sister and my brother. Can you help me understand now?" Aluel spoke up.

"Listen now, Aluel. I think the natural sciences are meant to explain the physical, and that's you in this example. You know the fact that you're a physical being, right? That's the half of you. The spiritual part of you is invisible, therefore, it can't be studied in a human way. You can't detect and then examine a spirit. It's like the win, and I think this is what Jesus meant when he told Nicodemus that those who come from God are like the wind. We can feel and hear the wind blows, but we can't tell how far it has travelled and how far it's going to travel before it comes into a stop. Do you now see the point? We can't study the spirit, but that doesn't mean it doesn't exist. In fact, when we die, we cease to exist. That means we've left our physical bodies. The real us have gone out of us," Nyaluak goes on with her heartfelt explanations, but will she convince the social critics?

"I agree with you, Nyaluak. This is what I meant by saying that the natural sciences explain the physical world and that the spiritual world can be explained in its own ways. You've just done that math. We can only study the spiritual worlds from within. And as you said, the physical world is the evidence of the spiritual world. But what has all this to do with the virus? Remember that we're still talking about the new virus. What is it and how can we overcome it?"

"Yes, we're talking about the virus, Mut. But Aluel thinks it's caused by spirits, which is false because we can't verify it either way. We don't know and there's no way we're going to know if it's true. I believe it was created. You seem to believe it's from the natural world. These two arguments sound true," Nyaluak explained."

CHAPTER 30

July 16th 2011, Rumbek, South Sudan

"Is regime change a solution or another problem?"

"Anything can either be a solution or a problem, depending on how you handle it. Regime change in some countries is the only way to fix situations, but this doesn't mean it will always work in the same way everywhere else. Look, if you're not careful, you're going to end up with the worst kind of genocide ever!" he explained.

"But many of our people think it's the only remaining solution. They think our leadership is always the problem. What can you tell them?"

"As I said, we have to be very careful. Don't forget that the government is the government. This means our current leaders are in control. They have all the resources and the armed forces on their side. Anyone trying to start a quo will end up in hell on earth, if not dead. I think violence is not the way to go at the moment. We've killed enough of our people."

"What do you think is the solution?"

"Again, anything can be a solution. But to answer your question directly, violence is another problem, not a solution to any current issues. The best way is time. Time is the solution. Time will come when these issues will be history," he explained. Right there, I didn't think I was getting it right. The old man sometimes uses parables instead of the normal ways of human communication. This is confusing, isn't it?

"What do you mean by the time? Do you think the situation will eventually get better and better by itself as the days go by without anyone doing anything about it? I don't think I understand your message here and I need your help."

"By the time, I meant to say that people still grow old and then die. Yes, we will all be dead and South Sudan as a country will remain forever as long as our people have a vision for it. Unless we go back to Sudan, we are but a country now, and this is my joy. I have done my part. Every martyr has done his or her part in the liberation of this country. Do you now understand?"

"Yes, I now understand you. But I'm wondering. How long do you think this time is going to come when peace and stability will reign in our country?"

"It doesn't matter how long that time will take before it comes into a realisation. It's much better than risking the lives of other thousands of people, just to get some other people into power. Listen, my son. Do you think that anyone going into power by force will serve the purpose? Do you think he or she will be there for the people of South Sudan? I don't think those who claim to lead the country for the people's sake will do just that whenever they get to power. Political power comes with its own issues and those who hate their leaders will likely fall prey to the same issues their leaders are facing or even worst!"

"Are you telling me that the new leaders will do exactly the same things the current leaders are doing or even worse? How do you know this?"

"Yes, that's exactly that I am after. I know this from our world history. People lure others into something for their own interest. Humans, especially political leaders, know how to get into power, and whenever they're there, they get stuck. Power means a lot in Africa. Do you know what our very neighbour used to say before he got into power? He thought he will get out of it at will, but the opposite is true."

"You mean to say our neighbour, Uganda?"

"Yes, you're right. President Museveni used to accuse his then leaders of overstaying on power, but what happened when he got there? You know the answers, don't you?"

"He wants to be there forever because he's serving his country and the people, right?"

"Exactly. But is he the only one to do this? He knows the answer, I believe. He knows there're others who can even do it better than him. But power means everything. It means you have all kinds of advisors to tell you what's right and what's wrong. Sometimes, these advisors are the actual leaders in any country. They can't just let it go, especially when the opposition seems to have a different agenda. It's easier to think one can leave power before they get in. But when they're there, they know it's not that easy."

"Power means everything?"

"Yes, it means everything in Africa. It means owning the country and its resources. When you're a president, you have all the resources of that country. The country is like your family and you're the husband and the father. You're the head of the state as they say. You're the symbol of that country. You can now see what I mean by saying it means everything. This means if you're a president in South Sudan, you own the oil revenue because you decide what to do with it. You can use the money to develop the country, or develop yourself."

"But is it right to own the oil revenue that's for a country and then use it as you wish when you're the head of state?"

"I don't know what you mean by the word, 'right,' in this context. But is there anything right in this world? Is there anything fair? Well, the answer depends on the situation, not on who we're asking. Even the so called humans rights have their own agendas and interests after them. It might be right for the president to kill anyone who wants to challenge him or her in the name of the country itself. In this case, it's right to own the oil revenue for the country, if the president and his group thinks so. They can either use it to develop themselves or the country."

"What if they use the oil money to build themselves as it is happening everywhere on earth?"

"You're right. They do use it for themselves, and this is called corruption in the West. This is why they love China so much over the US, or the West. Americans will love to know what the leaders are doing with the oil money. But China is different. China will care less about your part of the money. All they care about is giving them their portion. In fact, they can even dump the poisonous remains of the crude oil in the open air, if you allow them. It's your country by the way, not theirs. You decide. You have the freedom."

"What if the next president is going to sign a new contract with America, will that not be better for our country and our people?"

"Yes, this is our dream. But how do we know he or she will do just that? What if she comes up with revenge, especially if she's from a marginalised tribe? Don't you think genocide is possible in a country like South Sudan? I think we have to be careful since we can't tell what's in a person's heart until they show it. And we can't know they will show it until they are in power. And when they are in power, it's too late. We'll then keep weeping for yet other thirty years or so before another group comes to power. This is a cycle. It's not a solution but instead it's another problem to face. Let's wait. Time will come when this will be history."

"But can we make that history happen?"

"We can. We will. We always make history happen whether we like it or not. Son, life is not in our hands. I can't stop the quo from happening. Even the president can't stop that from happening. But if you're asking for my opinion, I am not a fan for a quo in any country, especially in South Sudan where it's much easier to make people follow people on tribal bases, not on any political ideologies."

"Is regime change possible without a genocide?"

"Yes, in the developed countries, and no in South Sudan. I have already told you what I think about this in our context. In our case, anything turns tribal in seconds. It might be a political difference between political parties, or persons, but it can turn tribal based on who these people or parties are. In this case, we can't manage to make a power switch without bloodshed. Therefore, we must be very careful about this. We have to count the cost. But if the new president is from any other tribe apart from being a Dinka or a Nuer, I think there will be a different story altogether, he said. "What if the president is an Equatorian?" I asked. "That'll be the best thing that could ever happen to this country and her people. This is because Equatorians are peaceful and educated more than us in both the Upper Nile and Bahr el Ghazal combined. But the question is how can we do this when we're still hungry for power? Can a minor tribe get to power in Africa let alone South Sudan?"

"What if we do it through the ballot instead of the bullet? Do you think we can be able to elect an Equatorian into the presidential seat?"

"Yes, we can do this, but will we? At the moment, we can't elect a person from any other political party into the presidential seat rather than those from the SPLM for many reasons, let alone someone from another minority group."

"When do you think we will arrive to that level?"

"I can't tell when. But when we're educated enough, we will be able to pass this level. We will then be able to judge issues correctly. But currently, all our people know about is tribes. The two major tribes are always in a fight of some kind. This fight can be in any institution such as churches, schools, and political arenas. This is serious, my son. You have to understand how tough it is to replace a president in Africa because being a president means a lot. It means your tribe always rallies behind you for the best national positions and the national cake. It's not just you and your country. It's not you and your family. It's always you and your tribe. Your tribe, depending on how big it is, will elect you in to power. It will also make sure it keeps you on power until you pass on, and it will then elect yet another of your kind from the same tribe. This is how hard it is to become a president in Africa, no matter how good you might be if you come from a smaller tribe."

"Are you scared of our current leaders?"

"I am not scared of anyone. I am old enough even though I am not yet ready to die. But I am telling you the truth as far as my knowledge is concerned. I don't know when you're going to be able to elect a president into power without ridging elections. Those on power always come back to power after those elections. This is common in Africa. This is also common in the East. One of the good things from the West is about electing leaders into power. The West understands what leadership is. Leaders are civil servants. The general public elects them into power and they have to be in power for a given period of time. When their time is up, they must leave. But this is never the case in Africa, is it?"

OTHER BOOKS BY JOHN MONYJOK MALUTH

From the year 2012 to 2022, John has written and independently published books and booklets under multiple series. He published these titles on Amazon and on other retail and book distribution platforms available to him. He is a nonfiction motivational teacher. Writing for him is one of the best ways to share knowledge before one expires.

1. SELF-PUBLISHING (10 BOOK SERIES)

Self-Publishing is a book series by John Monyjok Maluth, which is your best place to find relevant books that will help you learn how to write better, self-edit, self-design, self-publish, self-market, and how to get paid for your books by Amazon and other book publishing sites such as Smashwords and more. Use these books to your advantage. Read them to get published, today!

Series link on Amazon:
https://www.amazon.com/dp/B08N1MDB4R

Book #1: The Writer's Guide 101

The Writer's Guide 101 is a self-help guidebook for those who want to write but are still in procrastination mode. It will take you through the benefits of being a writer in our time and age in the world of advancing technologies.

Yet, you have to be a writer at heart. Do you wonder whether you are a writer? Most people share a common wish in life—ever wanting to write a book or two. Read this book today and make the final decision. However, it's not a step-by-step guide on the actual writing process. Rather, it helps you discover if you are a writer or not.

After reading this book, you will:
- Explore general writing misconceptions.
- Choose the right writer mindset.
- Understand writing types and how to choose the right genre(s).
- Learn from history and how technology improves our writing careers.

- Discover the writing best practices and how they work.
- Integrate these best practices into your own writing process.

Whether you are thinking or you have already written something, you are in the right place. This book is here to help you from the starting point to the finishing line. Read it to get prepared for your writing project. Take action, now!

Available In: Kindle | Hardcover | Paperback

Book #2: The Editor's Guide 101

The Editor's Guide 101 is an indie author's guidebook on how to self-edit professionally before sending the book to a professional editor. The problem is that most indie authors face one **BIG** common stumbling block—book editing. Some believe that writers are not editors. Some take it to another level and think that you can't see your own mistakes. Whether you're thinking of self-editing, or you have already tried it, you're in the right place. This guidebook shared some of the best tips and tricks on self-editing. It will show you the process. It will guide you through the concepts and also give you advice and support in your journey of polishing your manuscript drafts.

After reading *The Editor's Guide 101*, you will:
- Discover the wrong book editing concepts.
- Learn about book genres and how this affects book editing.

- Scan through book editing history and learn from it.
- Learn how technology helps you self-edit like a pro.
- Discover book editing best practices and use some of them.
- Learn how to use these tips in your project with guidance.

This book is here to help you out. With today's technology, distance learning is no longer what it used to be, and so does everything else, including writing, self-editing, self-publishing, self-marketing, and getting paid online for your writing career. After reading, you might choose to become a freelance writer. Take action, now!

Available In: Kindle | Hardcover | Paperback

Book #3: The Publisher's Guide 101

The Publisher's Guide 101 is a self-help guidebook for indie authors. With the help of today's technology, you can do the impossible, yourself. You can write, self-edit, proofread, design, format, convert, self-publish, and self-market your books. The book publishing concept is already changing from time to time.

After reading this book, you will:
- Learn about book publishing platforms and how they work.
- Go through the book publishing process step-by-step.
- Publish your first book yourself and become an author.
- Explore book marketing tools and services available to you.

It is much easier than you had anticipated. Go through this book and you will soon be published, and you will love it. Make your hands dirty and become a professional indie author over time. Take action by grabbing a copy, now!

Available In: Kindle | Hardcover | Paperback

Book #4: The Marketing Guide 101

The Marketing Guide 101 is a self-help guidebook to help you on how to make use of the modern digital marketing tools and services for indie authors. After writing, self-editing, and possibly self-publishing your book successfully, you need to tell people about it so that they buy it if they want to. But this is a common problem most self-published authors face, individually. Some believe the lie—authors are not marketers.

Is this your situation?

Whether you are making a lot of sales already or not, you're in the rightful place.

After reading *The Marketing Guide 101*, you will:

- Discover many different book marketing concepts.
- Choose the right marketing mindset based on your genre.

- Learn from the book marketing history.
- Learn digital marketing basics and how to use them.
- Explore social media and how it affects book marketing.
- Learn book marketing best practices.
- Use these tips and tricks for your own book marketing strategies.

The best part is that you can take action, right now. This book is a practical guide that the author uses to market his books. The tools are improving and new ones are coming into the market. Learn how to make use of them by reading this book, now!

Available In: Kindle | Hardcover | Paperback

Book #5: Payoneer Payments For Kindle Publishers

Payoneer Payments For Kindle Publishers is a self-help guidebook on how to get paid after successfully publishing a book on Amazon. If you live outside the US, UK, Canada, and Australia, and you self-publish books on Amazon, you might be facing some payment-related issues, already.

Since Amazon doesn't accept PayPal or any other banks located outside those territories, you will find it harder (if not impossible) to get paid by Amazon after you have sold a few copies of your book(s). However, this book is the only available solution in a nutshell at the time of writing. There were no other options out there.

After reading *Payoneer Payments For Kindle Publishers*, you will:

- Learn how to apply for an author's payments account with Payoneer.

- Wait for the MasterCard as it is being processed and sent to you.
- Discover how to activate the card when you receive it.
- Complete or update your KDP account payment settings.
- Receive your first payments from Amazon's KDP platform.
- Make your first $25 by referring others (when they earn their first $100).

Being a user of the service himself, John is here to teach you practical steps. He is a happy self-published author, using this same payment service since November 2012 with no issues at all.

Start to receive funds through your virtual bank accounts after every 60 days from the time you make a book sale on Amazon, no matter how much. Say goodbye to checks/cheques and instead receive your money through Electronic Funds Transfer (EFT) system, today! Make your writing career profitable by not worrying about how to get paid by Amazon. Take action, now!

Available In: Kindle | Hardcover | Paperback

Book #6: Self-Publishing Experience and Tips for New Indie Authors

Self-Publishing Experience and Tips for New Indie Authors is an author's story of how he started publishing his books on Amazon to share his stories with readers. If you read it to the end, you will learn how the author encountered challenges along the way and more importantly, how he overcame them.

After reading this book, you will:
- Meet the author and allow him to take you through new places.
- Discover your voice and remain consistent as an indie author.
- Explore the main challenges the author faced and learn from them.
- Learn how to avoid common mistakes most new indie authors make.
- Get proven self-publishing tips and tricks and make use of them.

This book can't be wrong—get the valuable advice, now. You need this book for your self-publishing success. Its message is not a promise; it's tested and proven. Take action. Find your desired success in the world of modern writing and publishing, now!

Available In: Kindle | Hardcover | Paperback

Book #7: Publishing a Book on Amazon's Kindle Direct Publishing

Publishing a Book on Amazon's Kindle Direct Publishing is a self-help guidebook on how to use the platform to publish books in both print and digital formats. It guides you through the process from the start to finish.

It's of great importance to be a writer because we can only communicate our thoughts to a wider audience through writing. However, it's one thing to write and another thing to get published and make your work available to millions of readers worldwide. This is because publishing a book has never been that easy. Thanks to Amazon's KDP.

In this book, you will:

- Study Amazon's KDP website and learn how to use it.
- Have a good reason to publish a book, yourself.

- Explore the website features and its marketing tools and services.
- Learn book publishing process for Kindle, Hardcover, and Paperback.

In those days, you had to look for a good publishing house through an agent. It might take years if you're lucky to even get accepted. This list of gatekeepers included agents, editors, designers, marketers, etc.

However, in today's world, if you only know what to do with technology, self-publishing may be the best option for you. Find out how by reading this book, today. Learn how to publish your first book and earn an author title. Be the gatekeeper, yourself. Be in charge. Take control of your product, your book. Take action, now!

Available In: Kindle | Hardcover | Paperback

Book #8: Discipleship Press Publisher's Guide

Discipleship Press Publisher's Guide is a self-help guidebook on how to use modern tools, technologies, processes, and services to publish and market your books very easily. With the help of today's technology, you can do the impossible, yourself. You can write, self-edit, design, format, convert, self-publish, and self-market your books.

In this book, you will read more about:

- The independent book publishing industry.
- How to publish your books, yourself, step-by-step.
- Creating your own book publishing brand.
- Marketing your books in a modern way.
- Enlightenment and how it matters in book publishing.
- Our services and how we might be of help to you.

After reading this book, you can create your book production company. It is much easier to accomplish more in this world of today than you had anticipated. Enjoy the self-publishing benefits. Take action, now! Good luck in your journey!

Available In: Kindle | Hardcover | Paperback

Book #9: Author Training Guide

Author Training Guide is a self-help guidebook for indie authors, which combines four different booklets in one book. It is a step-by-step guidebook on writing, self-editing, self-publishing, and self-marketing, all in one package.

Many people believe only professors can write good books. But this belief is not near to the truth according to the modern world of technology.

Technology has changed a lot of things in a positive way in our modern world. Things that were impossible to do a decade ago are now easy to do with a simple mouse click.

Included in this package are:
- The Writer's Guide 101
- The Editor's Guide 101
- The Publisher's Guide 101

- The Marketing Guide 101

Read this book to discover those concepts, which incite fear in new writers, and learn how to overcome them, personally. This book gives you the courage to move on from thinking to acting. After reading, you will learn how to write, self-edit, self-publish and self-market, and also how to get paid by Amazon after publishing and selling copies.

Available In: Kindle | Hardcover | Paperback

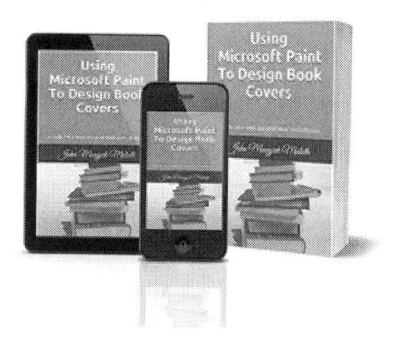

Book #10: Using Microsoft Paint

Using Microsoft Paint is a self-help guidebook on how to use the most basic and despised tool to create professional book covers for print and Kindle books. If you want to design your e-book or paperback covers using basic tools but don't know where to get started, here is how.

The book gives you a general overview of the software and then it teaches you how to use it step-by-step. It may be a wonder to use this basic tool, but creativity is not in the tool itself but in the creator's mind. You can even watch videos on YouTube for more tips and tricks on how to use Microsoft Paint to design book covers.

After reading *Using Microsoft Paint*, you will:

- Define what Microsoft Paint is and what it's used for.
- Explore all the features and learn how to use them.

- Learn how to create an e-book cover step-by-step.
- Learn how to create a paperback/hardcover book cover step-by-step.
- Explore other book cover design tools.

This guide is helpful to those who can't afford to hire professional artists or learn the complicated Photoshop to create professional book covers. Use it with your creativity and you will be ready to go. Explore the tool and then design your first professional book covers, your way.

Available In: Kindle | Hardcover | Paperback

2. COMPUTER BASICS (9 BOOK SERIES)

Computer Basics is book series by John Monyjok Maluth, which is mainly about computers: what they are, how they work, and how you can personally use one with ease. Learn computer basics today by picking one of these books. Modern technology applies to almost every part of our daily lives, thus, the need to learn how to use it for both personal and professional development purposes.

Series link on Amazon:
https://www.amazon.com/dp/B08NJW4HXY

Book #1: Windows 7 For Beginners

Windows 7 For Beginners is a basic computer guidebook for new computer users. It has advanced tasks, tips, and tricks for seasoned users as well. These tips and tricks will work for every edition of Windows including Windows 8, 10, 11, and the latest Windows versions afterward.

After reading *Windows 7 For Beginners*, you will learn:
- What Windows 7 is and how it is different from others.
- A brief history of Windows and what to learn from it.
- How to identify file types and filename extensions.
- How to configure Windows to connect to the Internet.
- How to work with Windows and other applications.
- How to fix common computer errors with ease.

Reading this computer basics guidebook introduces you to the world of computing skills. Make your hands dirty and enjoy the fun by learning new computing tasks and then work safely from home. Work from home is now a reality after the global pandemic.

Available In: Kindle | Hardcover | Paperback

Book #2: Windows 8 For Beginners

Windows 8 For Beginners is a basic computer guidebook for Windows users of all levels. It was written to make the transition from earlier versions of Windows Operating Systems much easier and simpler for both new and seasoned users. If you want to know the main differences between Windows 8, XP, 7, 10, and 11, here is the right place to get started.

You need to stay up to date with information because computing terms, designs, and software functions change almost every year. Windows as an Operating System software has been changing since v1.0. The transition from software to the next is what confuses the majority of users.

After reading *Windows 8 For Beginners*, you will:
- Define what Windows 8 is and what makes it different from others.

- Learn how to work with Windows 8 in simple steps.
- Learn how to work with files and folders on Windows 8 and more.
- Get ready to upgrade to Windows 10 or the latest, easily (system requirements).

Written by a computer user who learns by doing, *Windows 8 For Beginners* is one of the best computer guidebooks out there for computer students of any level of knowledge and experience. It has current tips and tricks on how to do your work faster with fewer mistakes. Learn the tricks, now! Take action!

Available In: Kindle | Hardcover | Paperback

Book #3: Basic Computer Knowledge

Basic Computer Knowledge is a basic computer guidebook on what computers are, how they work, and how to use them. It teaches you how to work with Windows XP, 7, 8, 10, and Windows 11. It will guide you on how to use Microsoft Word, Microsoft PowerPoint, and Microsoft Paint. It explains in detail how to write academic papers academically.

Whether you are a student, a banker, a salesperson, a teacher, a writer, or none of these, you need to know some basic computing skills. You can do this with the help of technology itself.

This *Basic Computer Knowledge* book promises you to explore:

- Introduction to computers and how they work.

- Microsoft Windows editions and their different functions.
- Different computational tasks you can perform without a degree in ICT.
- Learning by doing as if you are in a physical classroom.
- Computing best practices and online safety for you and your loved ones.

Technology has changed our world positively. In whatever you do, you need this core IT skills, either for personal or professional reasons. The fact is that our world has changed, and modern technology applies to every aspect of life. Take action, now!

Available In: Kindle | Hardcover | Paperback

Book #4: Microsoft Word 2007

Microsoft Word 2007 is a basic computer guidebook on how to use this famous word-processing software. Whether you're a student, a teacher, a writer, a pastor, or you simply want to boost your typing skills, you need a tool like Microsoft Word. This book explores all the features of Office Word 2007 and it helps you learn by doing.

After reading *Microsoft Word 2007*, you will:

- Define what Microsoft Office Word is and what it is used for.
- Explore all the taps and their tab groups and learn how to use them.
- Learn the common keyboard shortcut combinations to help you work faster.

- Explore basic important academic writing tips for academic papers.
- Learn tips and tricks on how to use the latest Word versions.

This book is great for those who are using the Microsoft Office suits, such as Office 2007, 2013, or the latter. It is very helpful to those using Google Docs as well because the same features found in both tools are discussed in this book step-by-step.

Available In: Kindle | Hardcover | Paperback

Book #5: Ten Successful Ways to Keep Windows Secure

Ten Successful Ways to Keep Windows Secure is a basic computer guidebook on how to use Windows tools to fix common computer errors. Computer error-fixing is not a job for everyone. However, fixing these errors may not always be free. What if you can fix these errors, yourself? This is where *Ten Successful Ways to Keep Windows Secure* comes in handy.

After reading this book, you will learn:

- How to use a **Disk Cleanup** tool.
- How to use a **Disk Defragmenter** tool.
- How to Securely Remove **Unwanted Software**.
- How to use a **System Restore** tool.
- How to create a **System Repair** Disc.
- How to use a reliable **Third-party Tool**.

- How to use an **Active Antivirus**.
- How to work with a **System Configuration Tool**.
- How to use a **Troubleshooter**.
- How to work with **Windows Action Centre (Windows Security)**.

This book promises to ease your day especially if you want to fix those errors in minutes. It is super-easy to understand and follow the processes here in this book and then fix those errors afterward, yourself.

Available In: Kindle | Hardcover | Paperback

Book #6: Windows 7 Control Panel

Windows 7 Control Panel is a basic computer guidebook on how to customize your PC. These tips and tricks apply to all versions of Windows including Windows XP, Windows Vista, Windows 8, 10, and Windows 11. Learning how to use these tools will make you an expert in computers.

The categories discussed in this book are:
- System and Security
- Network and Internet
- Hardware and Sound
- Programs
- User Accounts and Family Safety
- Appearance and Personalization
- Clock, Language, and Region
- Ease of Access

Take your computer knowledge to the next level. This book is an IT course in a simple format. It will help you fix common computer problems. This could be your next career if you do it well. People will pay you to fix their computer issues. Good luck in your journey of reading and putting the knowledge to work. Take action, now! Grab your copy!

Available In: Kindle | Hardcover | Paperback

Book #7: Windows XP Professional Control Panel

Windows XP Professional Control Panel is a basic computer guidebook on how to use Windows XP customizer and settings. It contains current technology tips and tricks for those who love to use older operating systems.

If you're using Windows XP, this guide is your best friend. It gives security tips for staying secure online, even if you don't get official support from Microsoft.

There are ten main categories in the control panel, and all have been discussed briefly in a layman's language.

In this book, you will learn how to work with:
- Appearance and Themes
- Network and Internet Connections
- Add or Remove Programs
- Sound, Speech, and Audio Devices

- Performance and Maintenance
- Printers and Other Hardware
- User Accounts
- Date, Time, Language, and Regional settings
- Accessibility Options
- Security Center

After reading each chapter, you will be asked to test yourself. Learning through practice is always the best. You may need to keep this book near your computer as you perform the tasks.

Available In: Kindle | Hardcover | Paperback

Book #8: Microsoft Windows 7

Microsoft Windows 7 is a basic computer guidebook with advanced features. It was written with both beginners and advanced computer users in mind. In it, you will find out how to download, buy, install, or upgrade to Microsoft Windows 7, 8, 10, or 11.

In this book, you will learn how to work with the Desktop, Start Button, Taskbar, and then Files and Folders. You will also learn how to use Windows Control Panel features to customize your Windows PC.

The following are the main features you will learn to use in this book:
- System and Security
- Network and Internet
- Hardware and Sound
- Computer Programs
- User Accounts and Family Safety

- Clock, Language, and Region, and then,
- Ease of Access

In this book, you will learn how to work with Windows Update, Disk Cleanup, Disk Defragmenter, and Advanced SystemCare. These tips and tricks will help you learn how to work with Windows like a pro.

Available In: Kindle | Hardcover | Paperback

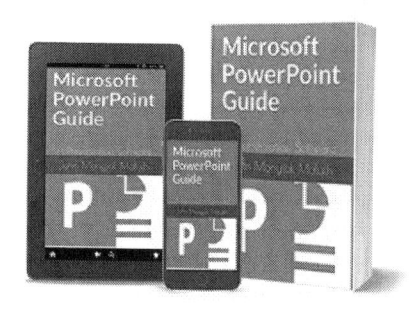

Book #9: Microsoft PowerPoint Guide

Microsoft Office PowerPoint is a guidebook about presentation software. We use this application software to create professional presentations and then share them with students or other viewers and audiences, depending on what we are doing. You can make presentations for your lessons or sermons, depending on what you do.

Below are the main points to guide you through this learning process:
- Learn how to work with the **Home** tab and its tab groups
- Learn how to use the **Insert** tab and its tab groups
- Work with the **Design** tab and its tab groups
- Learn how to use the **Animations** tab
- Working with **Slideshow** tab
- Using **Review** tab
- Learn how to work with the **View** tab
- Discover other **Hidden** tabs and their functions and,

- Learn some computing terminologies

This book discusses everything you need to know to create a professional presentation. In it, you will learn how to use those features of Microsoft Office PowerPoint 2007 and the latest versions of the software. Take action, now! Grab your copy!

Available In: Kindle | Hardcover | Paperback

3. SELF-HELP AND INSPIRATION (10 BOOK SERIES)

Self-help and Inspiration is a book series by John Monyjok Maluth and other authors, which contains motivational and self-help books. Use them to discover who you already are, (nature) and then learn how to improve your discovered self day by day (nurture). This is a long process. It will take time, but you will surely achieve the desired results if you persist.

Series link on Amazon:
https://www.amazon.com/dp/B08NK24L2B

Book #1: Academic Orientation

Academic Orientation is an academic guidebook designed to orient students in the academic world. This study workbook consists of research methods, learning techniques, reading techniques, and academic writing guidelines. Writing an academic paper is very different from writing an informal paper.

There are different academic writings and reporting formats also covered in this book. In the end, the students will be able to understand and practice the knowledge they have acquired on academic research and writing, both theoretically and practically.

The topics covered in this book are:
- Academic research methods.
- Academic learning and reading techniques.
- Academic writing guidelines.
- Using different referencing systems.

This study work is both **technological** and **practical**. It is technological because it requires technical work, and it is practical because each student must put these principles and techniques into practice. Master these academic research and writing methods today and you are ready to excel. Grab your copy now to get started!

Available In: Kindle | Hardcover | Paperback

Book #2: Freed Forever!

Freed Forever is a theological guidebook on how to find and maintain your freedom. Since we are made of spirit, soul, and body, we also get bonded physically, as well as spiritually. Thus, spiritual and physical bondage refers to the lack of freedom.

There is no room to argue about the presence of spiritual forces. The author personally knows that the spiritual world is real. He doesn't just believe it is real. He experienced it, himself. This is revelation knowledge, not gnosis or scientific knowledge.

However, we mostly disregard spiritual issues, or we simply confuse them with mental illness. According to this author, mental illness has many different causes, physical and spiritual depending on the case on check.

In this book, you will:
- Learn what spiritual bondage is

- Learn what physical bondage means
- Compare the two kinds of bondage
- Go through the freedom process
- Be free from all kinds of bondage, forever!

For this author, both physical and spiritual issues are very real. Not all mental illness is spiritual, and not all are physical. Read this book to understand the differences between physical and spiritual bondage. Find and maintain your lost freedom, today!

Available In: Kindle | Hardcover | Paperback

Book #3: Humans

Humans is a self-help guidebook with theories and facts about humans. We humans think differently, which is fine, natural, and very normal. But who are we? Are we apes?

The answer of course depends on whom we are asking. To a creationist, humans are not animals. Rather, they are special creatures, created for a reason, a purpose. To an evolutionist, humans are animals, evolving from other animal species.

However, all evolutionists don't share the same views. It's not all the evolutionists who don't believe in the creation theory. Also, it's not all the creationists who don't believe in some forms of evolution.

Can creationists become evolutionists? Can evolutionists believe in the existence of God?

Reading *Humans*, you will find:
- Introduction and definitions
- Human origin and races
- Human conflicts and their causes
- Learning from the past
- Learning from the present
- Learning from the future
- 50 Wise Words

The problem with the evolution theory is the missing link. It seems there is no scientific proof for macroevolution. The pictures we see in books are at best the artist's designs to illustrate how humans evolved from ape-like creatures, which resemble them in many ways. However, microevolution is confirmed.

Available In: Kindle | Hardcover | Paperback

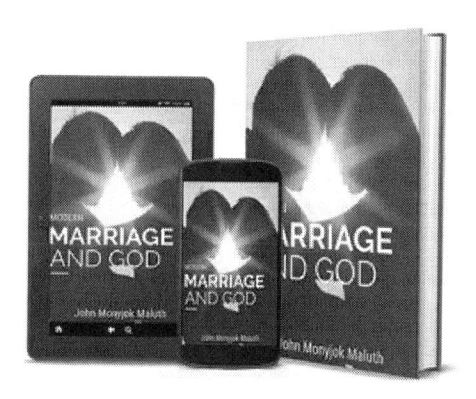

Book #4: Modern Marriage and God

Modern Marriage and God is a self-help guidebook on the meaning of true marriage in our modern world. Marriage, like any other human institution, has changed and is continuing to change its meaning from time to time. If you want to know more about marriage in South Sudan, here is the book.

In the newest country in the world, much is new, but not everything. Some ceremonies of long ago are still practiced while new traditions are being forged.

In *Modern Marriage and God*, you will read about:
- The traditional marriage process in South Sudan
- How other marriage processes are being introduced

- The changes taking place in the ways of marrying
- The reasons for 'modern marriage' being common
- Loving your spouse as yourself
- What true marriage means regardless of the process in use

In this book, the author compares each kind of marriage with marriage as seen in the Bible. His main purpose is to encourage readers to make their marriage true regardless of how it began. The book points the readers to a world of discovery.

Available In: Kindle | Hardcover | Paperback

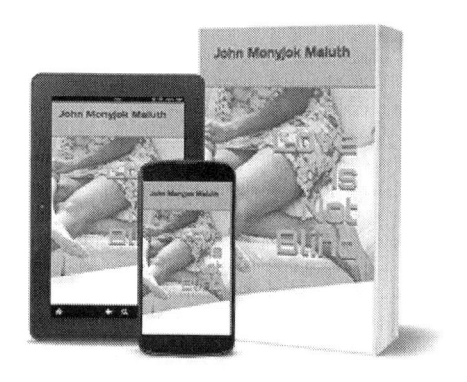

Book #5: Love Is Not Blind

Love Is Not Blind is a self-help guidebook, written in a literary nonfiction format, which carries the author's views on the misuse of the phrase, Love Is Blind, thus the title of the book. The belief that love between opposite sexes is always blind is a common false statement according to this modern world author. If love is indeed blind, then it isn't love.

Philosophy, science, and religion, are intertwined in this masterpiece. The book argues that most women don't feel what most men feel on our modern streets. This explains why men use terms that always mean something very different to most if not all women.

In reading *Love Is Not Blind*, you will find:
- The short fictional dialogue
- Males are not females

- Does he love you?
- Love vs Lust
- Conclusion

Read these conversations about true love and judge what it is and what it isn't. They represent both men's and women's views about human romantic love. Take a journey of self-discovery with these fictional characters to discover far beyond what you know.

Available In: Kindle | Hardcover | Paperback

Book #7: Affiliate Training Guide

Affiliate Training Guide is one of the best how-to guides for affiliate marketers, especially in the digital world. The main examples of genuine affiliate marketing programs and companies as discussed in this book are: Amazon Associates Program, Avangate Affiliate, Payoneer, and Wealthy Affiliate.

However, there are hundreds of thousands of multi-level marketing programs online nowadays, and some are not legitimate. Read this book to learn step-by-step how to find a legitimate program, which will help you work from the comfort of your own home, especially if retired.

In the *Affiliate Training Guide*, you will find:
- Amazon Affiliate Program (Amazon Associates)
- Avangate Affiliate Program
- Payoneer Affiliate Program

- Wealthy Affiliate Program

Read this book to get the most important information and to avoid scams and other security issues when trying to find a reliable second income-generating system online. Take action, now. Grab your own copy and learn how to earn just as the author does!

Available In: Kindle | Hardcover | Paperback

Book #8: Internet Residual Income

Internet Residual Income is an online business self-help guidebook. It will help you choose the right affiliate marketing model that you can master. The author is an online business owner who is here sharing with you how he does it for the last 9+ years.

From scammers to spammers, the Internet is home to good and evil folks. Are you wondering how to find a legitimate online business? Are you unsure whether these things are real? You are not alone. People are afraid of technology in general and the Internet in particular.

After reading *Internet Residual Income*, you will:
- Define legitimate network marketing systems
- Explore the best online affiliate marketing sites

- Learn digital marketing basics
- Choose the right programs and use them
- Read about the in-depth self-publishing steps
- Write and publish a novel to earn a living

With this book, you're in the right place. Reading it will resolve your doubts about what you can accomplish with the help of technology—making real money, doing real things.

Available In: Kindle | Hardcover | Paperback

Book #9: The Y-Questions

The Y-Questions is a self-help guidebook, a collection of some tough real-life questions that are yet to be answered, if at all. These are natural in the sense that they are about all that the author could question at will. Our world, ancient, modern, and/ or eternal is full of everything that spells *wonder*. Thus is the man's quest.

Some of the questions are:
- Why limited identities?
- Why borders?
- Why life?
- Why death?
- Why conflict?
- Why heaven?
- Why hell?
- Why God?

- Why Satan?

In this book, you will be encouraged to question everything our religion and human traditions call 'truth.' As we keep learning, our minds are open enough to make us feel courageous to rethink our thoughts, rephrase our words, and redo our actions. Learning is never done until we exit the planet to the world unknown.

Available In: Kindle | Hardcover | Paperback

Book #10: African Polygamy

African Polygamy is a self-help guidebook on the subject of polygamy. To many, polygamy refers to men having more than one legal wife at the same time. But to the real sense of the term, the word refers to the state of marriage to many spouses, and this means a man or a woman can be described as being polygamous if he or she got married to more than one spouse at the same time.

Reading *African Polygamy*, you will learn:
- Why do most men on earth prefer polygamy over monogamy?
- Why the author became a polygamist?
- What life looks like in an African polygamist family?
- What role do our personality traits play in a marriage?
- The lessons in a polygamous life

- The author's advice to young and unmarried people
- The author's advice to monogamists
- The author's advice to polygamists
- General life lessons from the author
- Quotes against and quotes for polygamy

Read this book to learn more about the subject. It's true that polygamy is not soon going away, especially in places like Africa, but why? Why is it true in the 21st century that most men all over the world prefer having more than one wife at the same time? The answers to these important questions are found in this book: a true polygamist's story.

Available In: Kindle | Hardcover | Paperback

4. NATIONALISM (5 BOOK SERIES)

Nationalism is a book series by John Monyjok Maluth and Elly Lugwili, and it contains books about what it means to be a patriotic and a God-fearing citizen of any nation. These books are mainly about South Sudan and its land, resources, and people. Read them to help you become a better citizen in your own country and in the world. We wish these titles will be a part of your personal and professional development process.

Series link on Amazon:
https://www.amazon.com/dp/B08N2YT6DB

Book #1: The Principles of Conflict Management

The Principles of Conflict Management is a guidebook on nationalism. Human conflict is real and most people have their thoughts about what it is, its types, causes, and effects. This book has answers to the above questions on the root causes of conflict both ancient and modern.

After reading *The Principles of Conflict Management*, you will:
- Redefine conflict in simple terms
- Learn the common causes of conflict
- Explore the current national conflict in South Sudan
- Understand the main consequences of conflict
- Discover the conflict management best practices
- Learn how to prevent, avoid, or resolve conflicts

Conflict, whether tribal, economic, political, or religious, must be understood before any resolutions are reached. *The Principles of Conflict Management* is here to guide you through different conflicts and how to effectively manage them. Grab your copy, now!

Available In: Kindle | Hardcover | Paperback

Book #2: Our National Heritage

Our National Heritage is a self-help guidebook on nationalism. It's not only about the national resources, even though these are still our heritage. It's mainly about the people of South Sudan and their land, including its natural resources. When you ask a South Sudanese living elsewhere about his or her identity, the answer is obvious—South Sudanese.

However, when you ask the same person when at home, he or she points you to a region, state, county, Payam, Boma, and the list narrows down endlessly to family, sub-clan, clan, etc. But, what makes a South Sudanese? Is it by birth, application, or acquired citizenship? Is it color, language, religion, or ancestry?

After reading *Our National Heritage*, you will learn more about:

- Types of freedom and what it means to be free at last
- What love is and what it takes to love your country
- Redefining South Sudan and what makes one a citizen
- Thinking beyond a household, clan, sub-tribe, and tribe
- Common world views and how to choose rightly for yourself
- The brief human history and what to learn from it
- 50 wise words to integrate into your wisdom system

This book carries the voice of a patriotic writer. Free from political pollution, it represents the beauty of God's blessed land—the Republic of South Sudan. Read it and think bigger and become wiser. Read it and live in peace with God, yourself, others, and with the rest of creation. Explore the world of positive thinking. Love yourself. Love your country.

Available In: Kindle | Hardcover | Paperback

Book #3: Thinking Bigger and Wiser

Thinking Bigger and Wiser is a guidebook on nationalism, briefly taking readers through the history of South Sudan from the two main civil wars. The independence of South Sudan was a great achievement for the South Sudanese people. However, the following events keep bringing many questions to the thinking minds.

In *Thinking Bigger and Wiser*, you will read about:
- South Sudan
- The People of South Sudan
- Religions in South Sudan
- Education in South Sudan
- Thinking Bigger and Wiser
- Conclusion

People have been looking for real causes of the civil war, but no one seems to get the right answers. This book isn't trying to provide any answers because looking for criminals is not the point. More atrocities are being committed. We better find peace now and then look back to find out the root causes. Read it to think beyond your tribe.

Available In: Kindle | Hardcover | Paperback

Book #4: The Patriotic National

The Patriotic National is a guidebook on nationalism and patriotism. Many people in this country (South Sudan) may end up thinking that the whole world knows about South Sudan until the day they travel. One of the things they will have to notice from Uganda in the south, Ethiopia in the east, and Central Africa in the west is the fact that many people have very little knowledge about this great nation.

In *The Patriotic National*, you will read about:
- What Is South Sudan?
- The Civil War
- The Negative View
- The Positive View
- Conclusion

Since July, 9th, 2011, South Sudan is no longer referred to as **Southern Sudan** or **Sudan**. It's known as the Republic of South Sudan—RSS after the long struggle for freedom. It became the newest nation in the world as it consists of 64 African tribes with different worldviews and religions.

Available In: Kindle | Hardcover | Paperback

5. CREATIVE NONFICTION (6 BOOK SERIES)

Creative Nonfiction is a book series by John Monyjok Maluth, which is also known as literary nonfiction or historical nonfiction. The books in this series will help you learn from the author's life experiences, how those experiences shaped his life, and how you can personally use the same lessons for your own personal and professional development purposes.

Series link on Amazon:
https://www.amazon.com/dp/B08NJZV7XK

Book #1: Life Cure

Born in the Republic of Sudan at the beginning of the longest African civil war, Panyim entered the world of uncertainties, not knowing whether to turn to the left or to the right. The outrageous civil wars, the looming famines, the unavoidable hunger, the debilitating diseases, and the unknown destiny, were life-threatening.

However, there was a glimpse of hope.

In his heart, life was a journey that living things must take, whether they like it or not. Everything born must live before it dies. But, is this cure for life? Could there be a better option? With all the challenges mingled with hope, hidden deep inside his inner being, will there be a resolution? When is the civil war ending with all the suffering?

Frustrated, discouraged, and powerless, he faced it head-on. Life Cure is a painful, regretful, and unforgettable story of Panyim. Experience Panyim's cruel world as he takes you places.

Available In: Kindle | Hardcover | Paperback

Book #2: Beyond Religion

Beyond Religion is a story of Kiden, a woman character, searching for the meaning of life and love in religion. Born and raised in a multi-religious, multi-cultural society, Kiden was not living in her own world.

Like any of us, she lived among her people with her siblings, parents, neighbors, and friends. She had schoolmates and colleagues. She resided in a real physical world, in a great city, well known all over the world.

Available In: Kindle | Hardcover | Paperback

Book #3: Beegu City

Beegu City is an anthology of short stories written from the West Turkana District in northwestern Kenya. These short distinct stories deep dive into what it means to become an expatriate in a foreign land. They expose several events of suffering and hope. They are real stories though they carry with them the artist's voice.

Noxious snakes, venomous scorpions, creepy millipedes, inadequate food rations, unswerving sunbeams, and refugee life in general, set the saccharine stories apart. Beegu, a tamarind kind of desert tree, sits at the center of this masterpiece.

Life is a journey we must take individually, hence the aim of this artistic creation. Discover which African countries are mostly presented in *Beegu City*, a city made of thorny Beegu fences.

Available In: Kindle | Hardcover | Paperback

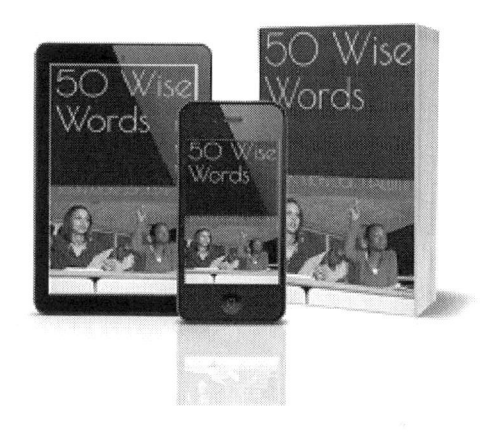

Book #4: 50 Wise Words

50 Wise Words is a modern proverb guidebook based on African proverbs, and it brings you 50 wise statements that have been classified as words of wisdom. These words will refresh your mind and memory. The book is designed for all reading levels.

Some of the wise words in the book are:
- Words are not insults in themselves
- The problem with misunderstanding lies in the miss
- Planning to kill time is planning to dismiss
- Our mindset controls our feelings,
- And much more...

Add these words to your list of wisdom words and your daily thoughts will surely improve. The book is excellent for readers whose English is the 3rd or 4th language. It is written in simple English. Wisdom is perceived and expressed differently, and thus, the Dinka and Nuer readers will understand these wise words much better.

Available In: Kindle | Hardcover | Paperback

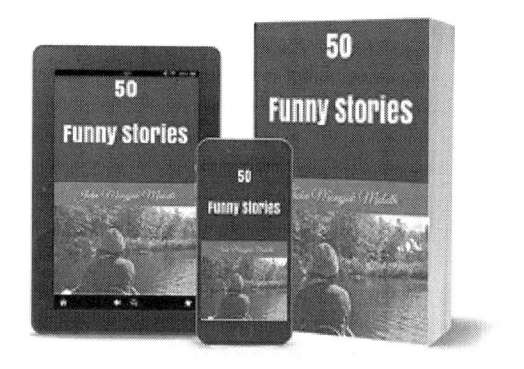

Book #5: 50 Funny Stories

50 Funny Stories is a literary nonfiction book on funny stories as far as they are read from the author's perspective. The short stories are not jokes or fables. It contains fifty (50) funny stories, some of which are real-life stories that will make you laugh out loud, thus the title.

For example, seeing a mobile phone for the first time, one couldn't believe he can use it for communication, or as it's called in the original language, a voice from far, telephone.

At least making you laugh is the author's dream, so that you enjoy this short life on the planet. Even though life is full of all it has for us, we are but to live.

Read it when you feel tired, lonely, or somehow depressed, and when you're in a quiet place. It will quench your thirst for fun, refresh your soul, return your lost joy, and redeem your happiness.

Available In: Kindle | Hardcover | Paperback

Book #6: The Bleeding Scars

The Bleeding Scars is a literary nonfiction novel based on factual stories for both Sudan and South Sudan. This makes the novel a masterpiece, a satire. Its stories are based on historical facts, though most were not written but oral in nature. This is the history of the then greater African country.

Read it to see how a nation could still bleed regardless of her coming out of the then perceived bondage and slavery only for it to enter into her own. Was it better for the South to remain under the leadership of the North? Is there anything like North Sudan? Is South Sudan part of Sudan?

In the nutshell, this novel helps its readers to re-think through their pasts in order to improve both the present and the future. With a better understanding, history won't repeat itself, but is this fact or fiction? Can the people of South Sudan live in peace and harmony without speaking negatively about each other? What's the role of an individual person in peacemaking?

Available In: Kindle | Hardcover | Paperback

6. MODERN POETRY (2 BOOK SERIES)

Modern Poetry is a book series by John Monyjok Maluth and other authors, which is the best place for you to find poetry books. Read these to feel the author's emotions and that of your own and get energized. Feel the energy and power of the written words. Poetry is still the best way of communication even in the modern world, and possibly will be for the world to come.

Series link on Amazon:
https://www.amazon.com/dp/B08NJYTLC1

Book #1: 2016 In Poem

2016 In Poems is a collection of the sweetest modern African poems by a South Sudanese author. Written from the Kenyan capital, reading these poems will make you feel the lovely weather.

These words will keep your soul fresh, renewing your spirit day by day.

These are poems of travel, weather, life, nature, and philosophy. In them, you will meet people, birds, plants, animals, insects, fish, and all forms of life known to man. Read it to positively reflect on life and its many issues and troubles.

Available In: Kindle | Hardcover | Paperback

Book #3: The World Within

The World Within is an African poetry collection of modern poems for life and its greatest questions. It contains 100 sweetest poems. These sestina poems are carefully arranged in six sestets. The inside world in every individual is a world he or she manifests on the outside only if certain conditions are met.

These poems promise to aid your curiosity as you devour them one by one until you are emerged into the poetry world before jumping back to earth. Read them today and share them with family and friends tomorrow.

Available In: Kindle | Hardcover | Paperback

7. CHRISTIAN THEOLOGY (13 BOOK SERIES)

Christian Theology is a book series by John Monyjok Maluth and other authors, which is the best place for you to find theological books and booklets. These can be classified into general theology, biblical theology, and practical theology. Use them to learn more about theology and other social sciences and their importance in our modern world.

Series link on Amazon:
https://www.amazon.com/dp/B08NJYG95H

Book #4: Synoptic Gospels

Synoptic Gospels is a biblical study coursework booklet. The term refers to the first three Gospels namely, Matthew, Mark, and Luke. Synoptic as a term comes from two different Latin words, meaning seeing together.

These Gospel books recorded the life of Jesus Christ on earth in a very similar ways, which means many accounts about Jesus and His teachings are similar in these first three books of the New Testament.

However, despite the similarities in the first three Gospel books, there are also serious differences in the same events. This is what Biblical Scholars refer to as a Synoptic Problem.

Read the Synoptic Gospels to explore:
- The Gospel according to Matthew
- The Gospel according to Mark
- The Gospel according to Luke
- The main themes in each book
- The Synoptic Problem and its effects

As a theological study course, this book focuses on Jesus, the Christ: prophecies, birth, life, teachings, and deeds. Reading it will help you know this historical figure in a better way possible as recorded in these books.

Available In: Kindle | Hardcover | Paperback

Book #5: Lifted Up For His Glory

Lifted Up For His Glory is a spiritual self-help guidebook. Humility is not being coward, afraid, or feeling ashamed. It's a divine character, given to us by the Holy Spirit. Mankind is a spirit being, a software, and is sitting in a physical body. Science in the real sense of the term means natural knowledge, clarifying that it can't cross the border to the supernatural.

We need the 6th sense to understand the spiritual or the immaterial dimension of life. It has nothing to do with primitive religious ideas from the past centuries. It has a lot to do with realities because facts are not realities. Facts can change whenever the newer ones show up. But realities and truths remain forever.

In *Lifted Up For His Glory*, you will read about:
- Humbled by the Spirit

- Justified through faith
- Exalted and lifted up
- Spiritual bondage
- Physical bondage
- Physical and spiritual bondage compared
- Bonded by traditions
- The freedom process
- Conclusion

This book is a spiritual guide for all. Depending on our earthly cultures, others may look down on us, or even say or do terrible things to us. Yet, if the Holy Spirit dwells in us, it will not be problematic to be humbled still.

Available In: Kindle | Hardcover | Paperback

Book #6: The Journey of Faith

The Journey of Faith is a personal narrative of a physical journey from Yei, South Sudan, to Lagos, Nigeria. The author discovered many things in the process, and this book is here to tell the story. The fact is that this journey began many years back in July 1997, when he gave his life to Christ Jesus at the age of 15.

The main points in the book are:
- The journey from Yei to Juba
- From Juba to Kampala
- From Kampala to Entebbe
- From Entebbe to Addis Ababa
- From Addis to Lagos
- The first Sunday in Lagos
- From Lagos back to Yei by the same route

It was indeed a very long journey, yet packed with discoveries and excitements. Meeting different people from all continents of the world, the author's dreams came to pass. As he explored the world, he learned a lot. He discovered more about life than being landlocked in one location. Take a tour of the author's world of discoveries, fun, and excitement. Get a copy, now!

Available In: Kindle | Hardcover | Paperback

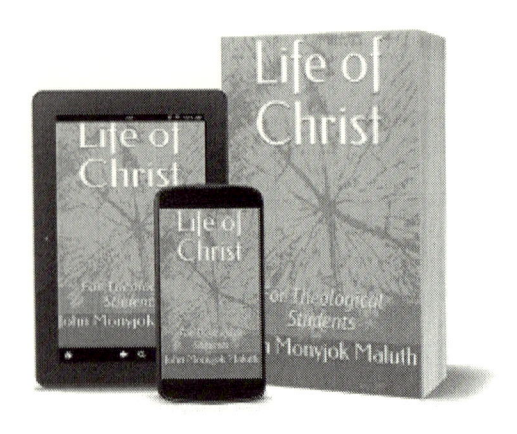

Book #7: Life of Christ

Life of Christ is a theological study guidebook, which discusses theological issues, not biblical ones. A theological study course looks at the spirituality of a biblical book or topic. Thus, Jesus Christ is a theological topic throughout the Bible from Genesis to Revelation.

After reading *Life of Christ*, you will read about:
- The 30 years of preparation
- The year of beginnings
- The year of gathering
- The year of opposition
- The Passion Week
- The 40 days

The study of Christ as a theological discipline is known as Christology. This coursework usually takes two weeks, using the modular format. The Life and ministry of our Lord and Savior, Jesus Christ, cannot be studied in two weeks. It is a lifelong journey for each one of us.

Available In: Kindle | Hardcover | Paperback

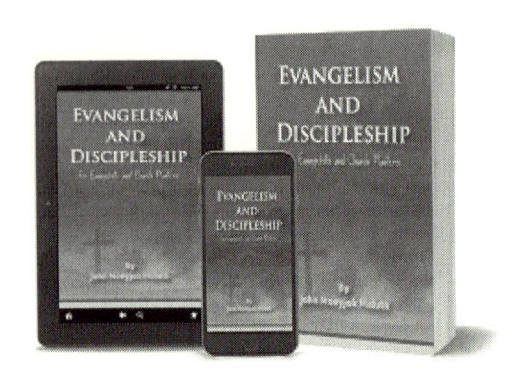

Book #8: Evangelism and Discipleship

Evangelism and Discipleship is a theological study guidebook that provides a brief study on the main ideas and issues in the field. These issues must be addressed in order for us to do an effective ministry of both local and global evangelization.

Adapted from Myer's book, this guidebook looks at:
- Basic issues in evangelism
- Barriers to evangelism and their solutions
- The message of evangelism
- Principles of evangelism
- Personal evangelism
- Public evangelism
- Crusade evangelism
- Follow-ups
- Evangelizing special groups of people

Evangelism and Discipleship must go together. Evangelism without discipleship is not evangelism at all. We can still bring people to Christ, but if we don't teach them to know who they are in Him, they will be like newborn human babies left in the jungle.

Available In: Kindle | Hardcover | Paperback

Book #9: The Book of Creation

The Book of Creation is a Christian philosophical guidebook based on the author's worldview. It does not argue on one thought or opinion concerning the correct view. It simply makes statements known to be correct according to the writer. These statements are based on revelation and scientific knowledge.

It never asks the reader to accept these views as if they are the only realities about our universe. It simply shares what the author accepts to be true.

In this book, you will:
- Explore different worldviews about our universe
- Get exposed to the invisible world
- Learn more about the visible world
- Explore the spiritual and the physical dimensions

- Accept you are part of the whole universe
- Love the world around you as you love yourself

Even though there are many conflicting views about our universe, and it's true that there will always be different views, it's reasonable that not all views could be correct. Pick the views in line with your personality type and live in peace with the world around you.

Available In: Kindle | Hardcover | Paperback

Book #10: Welpieth Ke Yecu Kritho

Welpieth Ke Yecu Kritho is the Gospel message written in both Dinka and English. According to the Bible, all people have sinned against God, but God loves everyone. This is the Gospel. God's Word says, for God so loved the world that he sent his only begotten son, to die on behalf of sinners. (John 3:16-17).

Reading *Welpieth Ke Yecu Kritho*, you will read:

- Introduction
- New Birth
- Righteousness
- New Life
- Satan's Lies
- God's Truths
- Conclusion

When people sin, it's not always about stealing, how they got drunk, committing adultery, or envying. All these are sinful, and they are fruits of a sinful nature, which is inside a human being. Read this book in both English and Dinka to understand the Gospel message better. God bless you!

Available In: Hardcover | Paperback

8. AUTOBIOGRAPHY (7 BOOK SERIES)

Autobiography Collections is a book series by John Monyjok Maluth and other authors. It has books about life experiences, travel, places, and the people met along the way. These books have a direct link to the general history of Sudan and South Sudan. Read them to learn from his life of trial and error, and to discover what it means to have faith in God even when life seems to be a nightmare.

Series link on Amazon:
https://www.amazon.com/dp/B08NJXG37Z

Book #1: Journeying with God Part I

Journeying with God Part I is the first book in the autobiography series. It's about John's childhood life, which includes events, his parents, and the places he visited as a child in the early 1980s. The stories are mainly from the 1980s - 1990s when. They are real-life stories, linking to the general history of his former country.

John went through hell on earth. You can see this through the lenses of his narrations of the same dangerous events in this book and in the books after. Since his childhood, he faced suffering, wars, inter-communal violence, and famines of all kinds.

In *Journeying with God Part I*, you will:
- Learn from the early events in the author's life.
- Explore the author's movements from place to place.
- Discover childhood events and their effects on his life.
- And then learn a lesson or two from them.

Born deep in a Sudanese village, it was impossible for him to go to school. Grab a copy now and explore John's world in this new edition.

Available In: Kindle | Hardcover | Paperback

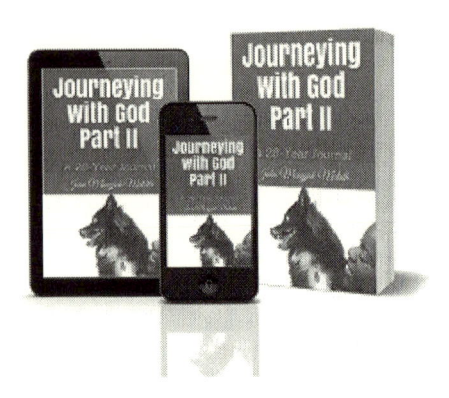

Book #2: Journeying with God Part II

Journeying with God Part II is the second book in the autobiography series. The author was born in Sudan in the 1980s, where he grew up in the village and saw the suffering of his people, first-hand. He faced famines, floods, wars, and inter-communal violence. In this second book, he tells the story of how he graduated from boyhood into manhood, and how he became a Christian, when, where, and why.

Reading *Journeying with God Part II*, you will:
- Start the journey where Part I has ended
- Explore the author's graduation from childhood to adulthood
- Learn how the author became a devout Christian, when, how, where, and why
- Discover the sufferings of the Sudanese people during the civil wars
- Learn more about hope and faith from the author's example

This book is a historical thriller in the shoes of an autobiographer. Read it to explore the world of suffering and pain then see how faith in God is stronger than any known life obstacles.

Available In: Kindle | Hardcover | Paperback

Book #3: Journeying with God Part III

Journeying with God Part III is the third book in the autobiography series. It's about how John started his educational journey under a tree in a war-torn Sudan in 1992 when he was 9 and the challenges he faced all the way through his university level. John has a story to tell.

Born in the Dhuording Village in the Upper Nile Region, John went to a church-based local school in the village. He started to learn how to read and write first in his mother tongue, the Nuer language. Like many other children in his day, he didn't go to school at the expected age.

Reading *Journeying with God Part III,* you will:

- Start the journey where Part II has ended

- Explore how the author learned reading and writing
- Learn how the author got trained in different fields
- Learn from the challenges he faced along the way
- Discover how the author started his writing career,
- And much more

This final autobiography book is a real historical account of Sudan and South Sudan in the shoes of an autobiographer. Read it to explore the two Sudans through these personal narratives.

Available In: Kindle | Hardcover | Paperback

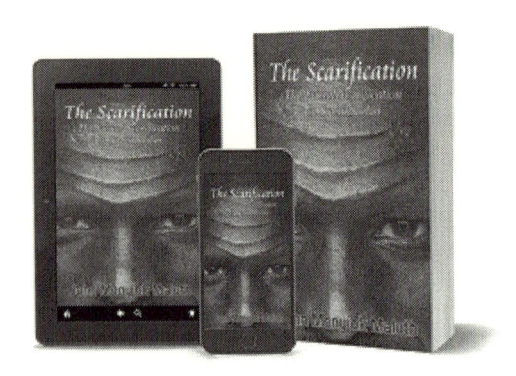

Book #4: The Scarification

The Scarification is the author's life storybook. It's about how he got his facial marks and what this means to him and his people. You might have seen someone with strange marks on the forehead and then wondered why and how was it done.

If this was so, then this is the right place to learn more about South Sudanese facial marks. You will learn what they are, how the marks are designed, when, and why they are important.

After reading *The Scarification*, you will:

- Explore the concepts behind facial marking in South Sudan
- Learn about many facial scarifications in different tribes
- Discover different views for and against facial scarification

- Learn at what age does it take place, in which season, and why
- Understand the author's arguments against this practice

Being part of his Journeying with God series, this book is focusing on one main event in the author's life. If you are working in South Sudan, then this book is your guide to introduce to you South Sudanese cultures. It introduces beliefs with their positive and negative effects in different communities you might likely visit.

Available In: Kindle | Hardcover | Paperback

Book #5: Journeying with God, Part I - V

Journeying with God Part I-V is an autobiography book that combines all three books and two more concepts in the autobiography collection series. John started his educational journey in the Nuer language in 1991/2.

In *Journeying with God Part I-V*, you will read:

- Journeying with God Part I
- Journeying with God Part II
- Journeying with God Part III
- The educational journey
- The war in Sudan
- The war in South Sudan
- Vision and mission

Read this book to learn how the author and his classmates started their classes using his cowhide, (the same one he sleeps on) as their chalkboard. It was pinned on a tree, so that a teacher could write on it, using a piece of charcoal. The students used the floor to take notes.

Available In: Kindle | Hardcover | Paperback

Book #6: Sudan Civil Wars and the Calling into Ministry

Sudan Civil Wars and the Calling into Ministry is an autobiography by a South Sudanese writer, who 'set out to show that God cares for His people, whether they know it or not,' (from the introduction). It begins with Sudanese wars, for the writer was born as the war began.

Chapters 2-4 are about his parents and memories of his rural childhood. Chapters 5-13 are about learning. His formal education began with a few months here and there in "bush schools" run by volunteer teachers.

Another Teacher came into his life when he responded to the Good News of the New

Testament. The Holy Spirit taught and shaped him, as he lived through grievous hardships.

In chapters 14-19 the author tells how a vision for ministry inspired him to struggle for a university degree, and so be equipped for his calling.

The last chapter invites readers to be peacemakers 'to see all the South Sudanese people united in worshipping the only true God' (Chapter 20).

Available In: Kindle | Hardcover | Paperback

9. PERSONAL DEVELOPMENT (7 BOOK SERIES)

Personal and Professional Development is a book series by John Monyjok Maluth on how to discover and then gradually improve both yourself and your career. The first two books in the series focus on personal development, while the last two focus on professional development. If you need some professional tips on self-discovery, self-improvement, career discovery, and career improvement, these books are for you. Read them in that order and see the results.

Series link on Amazon:
https://www.amazon.com/dp/B09FQ6JN77

Book #1: Your Self Discovery Guide

Your Self-Discovery Guide is a personal development guidebook for those who want to discover their personality types in order to live fulfilled lives. Humans, created or evolved, have individual characters, behaviors, likes, and dislikes. Whether people call you names, you are who you are, naturally.

After reading *Your Self-Discovery Guide*, you will:
- Explore the realities of the material and the immaterial dimensions
- Be guided on how to redefine your career, gifts, and talents
- Learn how to wisely put these truths to work
- Get advice on having the right mentors and peers
- Learn how to help others discover themselves
- Use the author's examples for your self-discovery processes

Reading this book will guide you through self-discovery step-by-step. How you define yourself makes you either enjoy this short life or lose everything in it. Read it to discover yourself and live in peace with yourself and with others around you.

Available In: Kindle | Hardcover | Paperback

Book #2: Your Self-Improvement Guide

Your Self-Improvement Guide is a personal development guidebook for the youth, as well as for anyone who has discovered their personality types and wants to improve that discovered self, gradually. This book is connected to the first book in this series, *Your Self-Discovery Guide*.

After reading *Your Self-Improvement Guide*, you will:
- Learn how to improve your self-image
- Learn self-improvement by reading the right materials
- Learn how to improve yourself by choosing what to watch
- Learn how to improve yourself by choosing what to listen to
- Learn how to improve yourself by doing
- Learn how to improve yourself from friends and mentors

- Learn how to improve your spiritual and physical entities
- Learn how to choose a life vision
- Explore and learn from 100 self-improvement tips and tricks

After reading this second book in the personal and professional development series, you will be able to improve your discovered self greatly. The 100 tips and tricks in this book will guide you through the importance of personal development.

The best way to improve your discovered self is to get a copy of this personal development book and read it today. Take action and learn by doing. It's possible to improve yourself instead of wishing to become someone else.

Available In: Kindle | Hardcover | Paperback

Book #3: Your Career-Discovery Guide

Your Career-Discovery Guide is a professional development guidebook for those who want to discover their best careers before they learn how to improve on them. This is the third book in the Personal and Professional Development series.

A career and a job are not the same in the sense that a career is what you love doing, while a job is what you may end up doing just because of other unwanted external forces to make the ends meet.

After reading *Your Career-Discovery Guide*, you will:
- Learn how to get exposed to your best career.
- Learn how to choose a career by learning more about what it is.
- Learn why and how to choose that career.

- Seek other people's opinions on how to choose a career.
- Choose a career in line with your heart's knowledge.
- Discover your career by making your hands dirty.
- Try different things to discover your career.
- Learn when and how to quit doing what doesn't work.
- Get a career choice from your peers.
- Choose the best career based on your mentors' advice.
- Explore and learn more from 100 tips and tricks.

If you have not discovered your best career yet, reading this book will help you think better. It will guide you on how to make the best career choices based on true knowledge. The best way to get started is to get a copy of this book and read it today.

Available In: Kindle | Hardcover | Paperback

Book #4: Your Career-Improvement Guide

Your Career-Improvement Guide is a professional development guidebook for those who have discovered their best careers and are ready to improve on them, gradually. It offers career improvement tips and tricks that will help you learn by doing.

After reading *Your Career-Improvement Guide*, you will:
- Evaluate and discover how far you have gone in improving your career
- Explore and learn from your career strengths
- Learn from your career weaknesses
- Discover your career opportunities
- Get exposed to your career threats
- Improve your career by reading more about it

- Improve your career by listening to the right messages
- Improve your career by watching the best mentors
- Improve your career through daily practice
- Explore and learn from 100 career-improvement tips and tricks
- Learn how to love your career heartily

To improve on your career, you first need to discover it. The best thing you can do to keep improving on your career or discover a new one is to get a copy of this book, read it, and then take action. Grab a copy now!

Available In: Kindle | Hardcover | Paperback

Book #5: Personal Development

Personal Development contains books 1 and 2 of the Personal and Professional Development series. These first two books focus on your personal development from self-discovery to self-improvement. Before you work on your career, you first need to work on your personality. What personality type are you? To answer this important question and more, read these first two books.

Your Self-Discovery Guide - this book takes you through the introduction part of the concepts later on expanded in the following books in this series. It has five main chapters. In the first chapter, you will learn what it means to discover your true self. In the second chapter, you will learn career/role discovery. Then you will be guided on how to accept these truths about you and your roles in the third chapter.

The fourth chapter will guide you on how you can put into practice what you have learned about yourself and about your career in the first three chapters. Then the fifth and final chapter tells you what happened to the author that changed his worldview and improved his life from then onward. Would this be helpful to you, personally?

Your Self-Improvement Guide - this second and last book in this collection takes you through the self-improvement process. How can you improve your discovered self? Here, you will learn that reading good books is part of the improvement process. How about learning how to write in any known human language? Does this help you think more critically about life and its issues?

Main Features
- 5 main self-discovery and career-discovery chapters.
- 15 chapters with 10 best tips each on each lesson discussed.
- 150 proven tips and tricks for your personal development.

Grab your copy today and learn how to develop yourself before you work on your career discovery and career improvement. This book is a tool in your hands to help you live a fulfilled life of your very own, not that of the society or group of people.

Available In: Kindle | Hardcover | Paperback

Book #6: Professional Development

Professional Development contains books 3 and 4 of the Personal and Professional Development series. These four last books in the series are meant to help you discover and then gradually improve on your best career, which is in line with your personality type. To discover and improve your personality, see the first two books in the series.

Your Career-Discovery Guide - this book guides you through career-discovery tips and tricks. Here, you learn the main differences between a career and a job, and why this is important for you, personally.

Your Career-Improvement Guide - this book guides you through improving your discovered career through reading, asking questions, and more importantly, doing your best activities each and every day as much as you can. Indeed, practice makes perfect as someone rightly said.

Main Features
- 20 distinct helpful chapters
- 200 proven tips and tricks on career discovery and career improvement
- 20 different great motivational and inspirational quotes from popular scholars and motivators
- Learning through author's real-life experiences, and,
- Much more...

Grab your copy today and learn how to work on your career, not your job. Your career is your hoppy turned into a business or service. It is what you do with leisure and not out of pressure. You enjoy the process and not the rewards or benefits ONLY.

A job can be whatever you do because of external forces such as money or survival. Become a free human today and do what you love doing, each and every day of your short life on earth!

Available In: Kindle | Hardcover | Paperback

Book #7: Personal and Professional Development

Personal and Professional Development contains books 1 through 4 of the Personal and Professional Development series. In this collection, you will be guided on how to develop your personality by first discovering and then gradually improving your personality type. Then you will be helped on how to discover and then improve on your career.

Personal Development - this section teaches you how to use self-discovery and self-improvement processes in order for you to work and build your personality. In this first section, you will be taken through proven tips and tricks used by successful people of both ancient and modern worlds alike.

Professional Development - this last section teaches you how to work on your career, which is also called or referred to by most prominent psychologists as professional development. Here, you will learn career-discovery and career-improvement processes that you might have missed out on from your previous schooling.

Main Features
- 35 chapters with valuable information on personal and professional development
- 350 proven tips and tricks on personal and professional development
- 35 motivational and inspirational quotes from well-known scholars and motivators
- Valuable personal real-life experiences from the author, and,
- Much more...

Indeed, life is the best teacher of all times, and some teachers called it, *learning through experience*. None of us can change his or her nature; yet, we are told or reminded to do just that, everywhere we go, including in churches and Mosques or Temples.

This collection of four motivational books is a tool in your very own hands. You can either use it or lose it all, today! Grab your copy now and learn how to do self-discovery, self-improvement, career discovery, and career improvement in a proper way.

Available In: Kindle | Hardcover | Paperback

FOR MORE COPIES, PLEASE CONTACT ME

Website: www.johnshalom.com
Email: info@johnshalom.com
Physical Address: PO BOX 28448-00100, Nairobi, Kenya.
Phones: +211 927 145 394
+254 797 624 994

Made in the USA
Middletown, DE
10 April 2023